A Glimpse
of Scarlet

ALSO BY ROXANA ROBINSON

Summer Light
Georgia O'Keeffe: A Life

A Glimpse of Scarlet

AND OTHER STORIES

Roxana Robinson

Edward Burlingame Books
An Imprint of HarperCollins*Publishers*

The following stories appeared in slightly different form in these publications:

"Snowfall" in *The Fiction Magazine*, February 1986; "The Time for Kissing" in *Atlantic Monthly*, February 1991; "Layering" in *The Fiction Magazine*, September 1985; "A Glimpse of Scarlet" in *New York Woman*, March 1990; "Second Chances" in *The Fiction Magazine*, June 1987; "Charity Dance" in *The Fiction Magazine*, 1986, and *Southern Review*, Winter 1987; "Daughter" in *McCall's*, November 1980; "Graduation" in *Wig Wag*, September 1990; "Getting On" in *The New Yorker*, March 1983.

A GLIMPSE OF SCARLET AND OTHER STORIES. Copyright © 1991 by Roxana Robinson. All rights reserved. Printed in the United States of America. No part of this book may be used or reproduced in any manner whatsoever without written permission except in the case of brief quotations embodied in critical articles and reviews. For information address HarperCollins Publishers, 10 East 53rd Street, New York, NY 10022.

FIRST EDITION

Designed by Alma Orenstein

Library of Congress Cataloging-in-Publication Data

Robinson, Roxana.
    A glimpse of scarlet and other stories / Roxana Robinson.
    p. cm.
    ISBN 0-06-016331-3
    I. Title.
PS3568.03152G5   1991
813'.54—dc20   90–84359

91 92 93 94 95 NK/RRD 10 9 8 7 6 5 4 3 2 1

This book is for
my best friend,
Tony

CONTENTS

SNOWFALL

@

During the Second World War, the American Friends' Service Committee gave my mother the name of a Polish woman whose family needed help. My mother wrote to her in English and sent her a parcel of clothes. Anna replied with pages of closely written blue script, in Polish. With it, in another hand, was a stilted and awkward English translation, full of formal, old-fashioned phrases. Anna's letters ended always, shockingly, "I give you hot kisses."

There were five children in our family, and nine in Anna's. Our mothers were of an age. They kept each other informed, though there were different milestones. My mother wrote about graduations, commencements; Anna had more exotic news: baptisms, first Holy Communion, saints' days, weddings. Sometimes—rarely—Anna sent us photographs, and we pored over the faces of the family we all knew. This was Zygmunt, who now wore, I could see, the torn green sweater I had outgrown, passed down to me third-hand, the hole in the elbow concealed by an innocent hand: these brilliant black eyes, awkward knees, cropped bristly blond hair. This was Margareta, the high forehead, square shoulders, soft, long ringlets. Anna's husband, Andrzej, looked, with his faintly pointed ears and questioning eyebrows, as though he were on the verge of a smile, but Anna was stern, her jawline strict. They faced the camera bravely, those black-and-white faces: set and solemn for the moment of record, their mouths firm, their eyes challenged, gleaming, their bodies frontal, backs straight, as though they were responding to some question about themselves. Here we are.

At Christmas, at Easter, Anna sent a Communion wafer in a small envelope. Thin, brittle, a translucent white, it had an image impressed onto its fragile surface. Propped on a shelf in our kitchen, the wafer was always surrounded by the artifacts of our more casual lurid life: photographs of our family, for example, snapshots, us lolling about; maybe the wafer would stand next to a small radio stuck there in a hurry, full of cant and chat.

For us, the wafer was as exotic as some Eastern amulet: Quakers have no such magic things. The wafer lay on our shelf pale and mysterious, the secret strength of it rising, spreading invisibly through our lives, faint and serene, subtle as scent. Once I ate one in secret, holding that faint, chalky presence on my tongue, pressing it, melting it, against the roof of my mouth, waiting, my eyes closed, breath held, for some mystical transference from Anna's life to mine.

Anna's letters were full of gratitude. We were not rich, and most of the clothes we sent were secondhand. I was secretly embarrassed for her, that she should be so pleased to receive things that were so patently out-of-date, so visibly used. In spite of those sober black-and-white faces, those careful poses, challenged eyes, I had my own vision of Polish life. It was brightly colored, full of fat blond braids, cottages warm with cooking, glittering officers on wild-eyed horses, red-stitched blouses, strange skies full of stars I did not know.

Those frail white wafers were symbols of that other life, made up of syllables I could not speak. *I give you hot kisses!*

Now one of Anna's children has arrived in America, and my mother calls me. It is Janusc, which sounds like Yanoosh. I remember him. Solemn, quizzical, large-eyed, he stood crookedly against his mother, wearing a sailor suit, short pants, neat collar. Nineteen forty-seven. He is now a house painter, and my mother wants me to hire him. Where would he stay, I ask. He'd stay with you, she says, it would be easy. But I don't speak Polish, I say, anxious. I think of mealtimes with this strange man, who will not be wearing a sailor suit now: I think of explaining spackle, latex paint, the dishwasher.

Janusc is staying with a cousin, who calls me. He speaks good English, and is very soothing. Janusc will be no trouble, he says, don't worry. Just give him a room and a TV and he'll be no trouble. I have no answer. It bothers me that we talk about Janusc as though he were a beast, an invalid, as it bothered me when we laughed at those stilted, awkward English phrases.

When Janusc arrives we all smile widely at each other, we shake hands ceremoniously. The cousin stays, while we go over the painting to be done, then says good-bye. Janusc is small, my own height, with a creased, narrow, mournful face. He wears heavy sandals, and a short plaid gray coat that ends above his knees. His hair, his eyes, the cast of his skin are gray. With his grieving eyes and quiet face he looks Polish; his somber coloring and old-fashioned clothes make him look like someone in a photograph taken during the war, Eastern Europe. We have seen that look.

Janusc settles down to work at once, changing into soft, worn jeans and an old shirt. He moves quietly, a gentle shuffle from time to time is all I hear, but he goes at our

3

raddled walls up on the third floor with great determination. We believe we have conversations with each other; that is, we each speak long and complicated sentences in our own languages, with much smiling and gesturing, but there is no way to determine that we are even talking about the same subject: I ask if he is ready for lunch, he answers that he will need more primer for the moldings. We believe that we understand what the other says, but this is not always so: poor Janusc paints the bathroom three times, in different colors, because of a mistake; mine, not his. I learn some useful words from his battered red dictionary: *yes, no, please, thank you, more, sorry, beautiful.* The sounds are strange and unmanageable. Janusc has his own set of strange words: *ceiling, paint, milk, bread, dog,* and *tea-China.*

At dinner, Janusc comes down in clean clothes, washed and shining. He sits with my husband, my daughter, and me at the small maple table in the kitchen, watching us with concentration if we try to speak to him, looking politely elsewhere if we do not. One night, after a bottle of red wine has been emptied by the three of us, he brings down photographs: his parents, his wife, Anna and the whole family when he was five, Anna and Andrzej today. They are all pictures I have seen, of course, and, sitting next to Janusc beneath the glowing lamp in my kitchen, I am as delighted to see them in his hands, at my table, now, as though we had suddenly broken through the barrier of speech, and our words and thoughts flowed in a limpid rush from one to the other of us. These faces are all old friends of mine. Have they not all sent me hot kisses?

Janusc hands me a photograph of himself in a dark suit, standing stiffly next to a woman in a white dress, with a cloudy white veil about her head. Nineteen sixty-two, Janusc says, I think, in a soft, sliding Polish. He traces the numbers

4

slowly on the tablecloth: one, nine, six, two. *Tak, tak,* I say, nodding vigorously, yes, yes. He has given me all I need to know, these two solemn faces, the moment, the date. I point to the face of his wife, who has melting, slanting black eyes, and a wistful expression. *Ladne,* I say, beautiful. Janusc smiles, a shift which transforms his face entirely from its somber verticality. It becomes imp-like, the mouth a deep V, the corners of the eyes slanting suddenly upward.

During the day it is difficult to remember that Janusc is in the house. He is quiet, there on the third floor, crouching on his knees now, filling in the cracks between the floorboards. I work at my drawing board on the second floor, in silence. At intervals we meet in the kitchen, or I go upstairs to him with a mug of tea-China and a slice of bread. He likes my bread, and I find myself baking three times a week, instead of once.

I am pleased to have him in my house: I wish I could send him back to Poland with some of our space, some of our vivid colors, the warmth of the house. I no longer believe that life in Poland is made up of those embroidered reds and complicated dances. Janusc and his family have had difficult times. I wonder what he thinks of us here. I find myself embarrassed at our casual plenty, at the huge quantities of food, of stuff, I seem to buy for our small family. Janusc himself is modest in his appetites, he eats and drinks sparingly.

But it is more than food. If the truth be known—and it will be known to someone who lives in your house, whose days are spent silently in your rooms—I do not use my time as well as I ought. Janusc never stops working, but I spend, listening to him sanding and scrubbing up there, some time staring out the window. And the time I spend working—I am doing a series of still lifes in pastel, a set of white bowls that change endlessly with the light, the shifting of the shadows and mysterious arrangings of colors that fall across them—but is this work? I hear the floorboards above me creak. And worse, Janusc sees my cleaning lady come in to scrub out my tubs, and one Saturday night he sees a woman come in to serve at a dinner party. He sees me leaving the house with my tennis racquet: I smile, and point to the clock to tell him when I will be back. But I am embarrassed.

I do not think he knows that I go running, I have tried to conceal this altogether. It seems indefensible, while most of the world hoards calories and energy, to be so arrogant, so deliberate in their dispersal. I sneak out of the house to run, going down the driveway with the dog in a casual, long-strided walk in case he is working near an upstairs window, not breaking into a run until I am down the road, already into the woods.

Now, this morning, there is a heavy snowfall. The landscape, when we wake up, has been transformed: virgin, mysterious, alluring. To her utter bliss, my daughter's school has been canceled, though my husband's trains are running. He leaves, and she and I settle down, still in our nightgowns, with our breakfast, in the window seat in my bedroom, to watch the snow outside. It falls like white lace handkerchiefs, in huge, dreamy flakes. On the third floor, Janusc has begun on the door frames and moldings.

At midday we decide to go out. The wind has dropped, and though the snow is still falling, the sky has lightened. I call up the stairs. "Janusc!" I say, and beckon. "Photograph!" Janusc understands me at once, and nods soberly. "Okay," he says, and begins to tidy up. When he comes down, my daughter and I are dressing; it is twenty degrees. My daughter puts on thick blue snow pants, green parka, knitted cap; I wear my parka and goatskin boots. I hand Janusc a wool cap and my husband's down jacket. I offer him boots, to go over his sandals, but he shakes his head. He asks me something about the cap, but I shrug and smile, I do not understand. Outside, I turn, and see that he is putting on the knitted cap in front of the back door, the glass in its top half reflects his earnest face. He is adjusting the cap, pulling the top half of it down, making sure that its character is reflecting its bearer's, that its curves are Polish, its creases Januscian.

Outside in the snow, giddiness rises. Loose, limpid whiteness surrounds us, insistent and confounding. It is drifting down improbably—from the sky itself!

"Over there," I call, and I gesture for Janusc and my daughter to stand by the back door. I run back, away from them, clasping the camera clumsily to my chest. My goatskin boots thud through the heavy snow, its soft density yielding slowly, cumbrously, against my legs. I climb the slanting stone steps and crouch beneath the bare little crab apple tree so that I can get the whole house in, the two of them at the back door. I want the whole house as a backdrop: I want Janusc to be able to take this back with him, proof that he was a part of all this, to show that there has been some bridge between our lives. And I want to implicate him: If Anna looks at our farmhouse and purses her lips with disapproval—three stories, for only three people?—I want her to see that Janusc had lived there with us, he had his own room in our house.

And I have color film in the camera, and I have given Janusc my husband's bluebird-colored parka, so that no matter what Janusc presents me with in the picture, no matter how earnest, how solemn, how dour he shows himself, he will not be in black and white. Some transference will have taken place. And while I cannot defend idleness, frivolity, arrogance, opulence, I do defend the bright colors of our life,

I defend whatever grace we have achieved. And perhaps, when they see Janusc in this brilliant blue, before the house he is living in himself, they might forgive us our idleness, our arrogance: they will see that Janusc himself has taken on our wild hues, for this moment.

I squat in the snow, taking off the lens cap, adjusting dials and meters. When I see the figures through the tiny silvery window, at first I do not understand. Janusc has crouched to the ground. I think perhaps he is adjusting his shoe, but he is saying something to my daughter, and I see first one of her padded blue legs and then the other appear on either side of his face. She is sitting on his shoulders, and he rises quickly, with great ease, like a dancer. He stands very straight and graceful against the white clapboards of the house, the dreamy snow shifting past him in the still air. Janusc, in my husband's huge blue parka, raises his arms, holding them out straight at shoulder height, proudly, palms up; so does my daughter.

Their two faces, framed in woolen curves, are neatly stacked one above the other, and with the raising of their arms, as though this were a sign, they both smile: brilliant, brilliant smiles, their arms lifted in that regal gesture, signifying, perhaps, merely great delight in being there, at that particular moment, before our white farmhouse, in that snow-muffled landscape, their bodies bold and vivid patterns against the frail white translucence that surrounds them, merely great delight: joy. I give you hot kisses.

THE TIME FOR KISSING

My mother never calls me, so I call her. I make the call on Sunday nights. She answers right away, and I know exactly where she is. She spends Sunday evenings in what is called the library, though it only has two bookcases in it, and those hold more plates than books. Mother sits in the flowered chintz armchair, which matches the curtains. Bacon the dog is lying on his green pillow next to her feet. The walnut table beside my mother holds an ashtray, a small porcelain Cavalier King Charles Spaniel, and her drink, which is Scotch. Next to her chair is a standing lamp, and her feet are up on the upholstered footstool, which also matches the curtains. On her lap is the newspaper, which is folded back to the TV section. She is holding a cigarette in one hand, and the TV remote controller in the other. When the telephone rings she is interrupted.

"Hello, Mother?" I say.

"Who's this?" she asks warily, unwilling to commit herself.

"It's me," I say, "Susannah."

"Oh, yes," she says, and if I say nothing, she pulls herself together and adds, "hello."

"How are you doing?" I ask.

"Fine," she says, faintly peevish.

Mother is seventy-one years old, and has lived alone since Harry died three years ago. When he retired they began spending most of their time in Southampton. They sold the big shingled house on the beach, where we spent our summers as children, and moved to this smaller one behind high privet hedges. When Harry died Mother sold the apartment in New York as well. At first she planned to spend a night or two in New York during the winter, but now she hardly ever does.

"What have you been up to?" I ask, "anything exciting?"

"I don't know what you call exciting," she says, touchy. "We had the Garden Club meeting on Wednesday. There was a bridge party at Wah-Wah's on Thursday. That's about it."

"How was the Garden Club meeting?"

"All right. Though I don't know how Bambi Johnson got herself elected president, the woman is the very worst executive I've ever heard of. Most of the members won't speak to her any more. She ruined the benefit last year, *single, handedly*."

"Well, at least she's good at something," I offer, but Mother won't have it.

"Good at what? What do you mean?"

"Ruining the benefit," I say, but I know she won't laugh, and she doesn't. My mother suspects my offerings. There is a pause, and I have the feeling that she has turned the television set back on, low, so I won't hear it.

"Do you want me to call you back?" I ask.

"What? No, why?" she says.

"I thought you might be in the middle of something."

"No, nothing a tall."

"Well, I just wanted to check in with you. We're all fine," I say, since my mother hasn't asked, "except the garden is a nightmare with all this rain. There are slugs all over the place."

"It's getting pretty bad," she says ambiguously; I'm not sure if we're talking about the slugs or something on her program.

"How's Bacon?"

"Bacon's *fine*," says my mother, animated at last. "He's right here at my feet, snoring his head off. Eats like a pig. Keeps me awake all night, and sleeps all day." She is devoted to the dog.

"The reason I called was to tell you that I'm coming out next week to see Linda, and I thought I'd spend the night with you." Linda is a friend I grew up with in Southampton.

"What day?"

"It would be Tuesday."

"All right," she says neutrally. "I'm out to dinner, though."

"That's fine," I say, "I'll spend the evening with Linda."

When I hang up, I go back into our bedroom. The sight of it is a relief: cool and spare and muted; there is no chintz in my house. John is already asleep, lying like a friendly boulder in our bed. He goes to sleep early, though it doesn't last: later, in the small, deadly hours of the morning he will be awake. But now he is fathoms deep, and I move quietly, turning off the light on his side of the bed. I go into my bathroom to undress, and while I brush my teeth I look at the small photographs on the wall next to the mirror. There are pictures of John, of our children, Nat and Amanda, my sisters, Kate and Joan, my friend Linda, a few other favorites;

they are like amulets, emblems of my life. There is one of Mother, taken at a party, years ago. She has her hands on her hips; she is wearing a rose-colored dress with big puffy sleeves, and laughing.

I climb into bed next to John. Our sheets are cotton, and solid white, not the scratchy flowered Porthault linens I grew up with. John's legs are warm and solid. I turn my back, get out my book, and press myself against the length of him.

My father was well-born, impecunious, and wonderful to look at. It is easy to see why Mother married him, and easy to see why she divorced him. My father talks with a little tiny smile hovering about his mouth: he is already charmed by what he is about to say. Most other people find him charming, too. My sister Joan told me that women used to call up and ask for him. Mother would say, "Would you like to leave a message? This is his wife." The other woman would say, "His *wife?*" In spite of my father's charm, he is hard to live with. He is now on his fourth marriage, and each wife is richer than the last. My mother was the first, and she had no money at all. When I was three, the fourth child, my mother divorced my father and married Harry Satterthwaite. Harry had lots of money, and we moved to a big duplex apartment on the corner of Park and Seventy-ninth Street.

We all hated Harry: me, my sisters, Joan and Kate, and even Ted, our older brother, though he pretended to be above our concerns. Harry was only ten years older than my mother, but when I was little he seemed from a different age. His skin looked as if it had been put in storage: his cheeks were smooth and ancient, as though their living was over, and he had loose, thick rolls of flesh underneath his chin. The top of his head was bald, with brown spots on it. There were deep gullies from his nose to the corners of his mouth, and his teeth were yellow. His clothes were beautiful: soft leather loafers, cashmere jackets, silky cotton shirts. A man called Edwards, whom we also hated, came in the mornings to look after Harry's clothes and polish his shoes. When Ted acted like a stinker Joan would ask him when Edwards was going to start coming in to look after his moldy moccasins, his torn sweaters and stained Madras jackets. This made us collapse with laughter, but Ted could not answer without either aligning himself with us or with Harry, so he would punch us.

One evening at dinner Harry said loudly, "There will be no more chewing with open mouths at this table." I was six, and had just recently been allowed to eat with the grownups in the dining room. We all preferred the big white-tiled kitchen, where we ate with Sally, the cook, when there were dinner parties. The dining room was large and gloomy; at the windows were tall gray curtains that swooped back halfway down, and the table was long and dark and shiny, with a glass chandelier over it. In the middle of the table were two silver pheasants, fierce and spiky. Still, it was a privilege to sit there.

When Harry made his announcement my mother didn't say anything, she went on buttering a roll as though she hadn't heard. She wore her light brown hair in a shoulder-length page boy, turned under at the ends and parted on the side, with a narrow velvet ribbon holding it smoothly in place. At dinner she wore a cashmere sweater over her dress, with the arms loose over her shoulders like a cape. Mother always had a certain look to her: slim and smooth and polished, her linen dresses ironed, her hair neat. It seemed lovely to me, effortless and silky, as though my mother, just by being, happened to be perfect.

We looked at each other out of the corners of our eyes,

and Joan kicked me under the table. Joan was three years older than me. She remembered living with my father, and she was unbelievably brave. She now sat up straight at the table, holding the heavy silver fork easily, and looked back at Harry with interest, as if she were going to discuss it with him. "Why on earth not, Harry?" she might say. I always felt as though Joan were a seawall between me and the waves, breaking the shocks for me.

"It's disgusting, and I won't have it," said Harry, gaining confidence. He picked up the heavy crystal glass and took a courageous swallow of Scotch. I watched his throat move as he swallowed. The lump in it rose sluggishly, suddenly bobbled, and then disappeared mysteriously, as his short neck vanished and he lowered his head. "You," he said, looking at me. I wondered if he knew which one I was. He often confused us, calling us by each other's names. Joan and Kate were the easiest to mix up, as they were close to the same size, and they looked alike, with their round faces, sleek honey-colored hair, and blue eyes. "Did you hear what I just said?" said Harry.

I nodded, fearful, but kept on eating. It didn't occur to me that I was doing anything to bring on this attack; Harry's temper seemed unrelated to the real world. My big linen napkin was on my lap, where it was supposed to be, my silverware was on the plate as I ate, my milk had not slipped over the rim of the glass when I set it down, but clearly I was in for it, whatever it was.

"Well, *stop* it." He glared at me. "Leila, do you see what that child is doing?" he said loudly to my mother. She glanced briefly up at me, and down again at her plate. It was pot roast and carrots. "Hmmhmm," she said, and addressed the meal.

"I am in *earnest*," said Harry, and leaned forward in his mahogany chair, gripping the arms with his hands. His chair and mother's had arms; the rest of us were left defenseless from the sides. Harry looked at me again, and I wondered what name he would use. "Susannah, leave this room," he said, and he waved his hand briefly, a high, short, weak wave, not as though he really expected me to leave. He looked down at his plate at once, and began sawing away at the pot roast. When he started talking again it was a sort of warning grumble, a retreating storm. "You can finish your meal in the kitchen, and don't come back until you have learned properly how to eat your food. It's disgusting, watching someone else's dinner wallow around in their mouth."

I didn't move, because I still wasn't sure what was going on, and he didn't sound serious. Harry looked up and saw me. "Didn't you hear me?" he said, and looked down the table at my mother again. She was staring with a look of intense concentration at an empty space on the table, as if she had gone mad.

"Can't find it," she announced. "Don't know how they lose it. There it is." Underneath the table she found the bell with her toe and pressed. The door to the kitchen swung open and Harry fell silent as Maureen came in. "Could we have some more water, in the pitcher, and I think we're ready for seconds, Maureen."

When Maureen left Joan said, "Mother, I—" and I knew she was trying to run interference for me, but at the same time Harry said, "*Leila*." He was really angry now.

"Susannah, you heard Harry," my mother said, without looking up. "Finish your dinner in the kitchen." I slid off the scratchy needlepoint seat and picked up the heavy plate carefully, trying to keep the carrots from rolling off.

After dinner I went up to Joan's room. Kate and Joan were lying on the beds, and Ted stood in the doorway, not committing himself.

"He's such a pig," Kate said. She was two years older than me.

"I am in *earnest*," Ted said querulously, and drank from an imaginary glass.

"Just pass me some more of that whisky," said Joan, "and I'll be even more earnest. I'm earnest and thirsty, all at the same time. I'm thirnest. I'm earsty." She threw herself back on her bed and let her tongue hang out, rolling her eyes whitely. "This is *really* earnest," she announced. She was still wearing her school uniform, a dark plaid jumper and a white blouse, and her green knee socks were rolled down to her ankles. Her loafers, which were scuffed and dull, hung moronically off her feet.

"Biscuit likes carrots," I offered. Biscuit was our big apricot poodle, who could be counted on to appear noiselessly under the kitchen table and dispose discreetly of unwanted items.

"Maybe he'd like Harry," said Kate, "maybe we could feed Harry to him."

"Ooof," said Ted, wrapping his arms caressingly around his stomach. "Poor Biscuit." This started us all laughing, and we began to imitate Biscuit making various responses to the offer of toasted Harry. While we were doing these hilarious things Mother came along the hallway, getting her glasses. She walked with her head slightly down, as though she were watching her neat small shoes, with rosettes on the toes. Mother was going back down to play backgammon with Harry in the library. She looked in at us but did not say anything.

"Hi, Mom," Ted said easily. He was her favorite. She paused and smiled.

"Having a good time?" she asked, and Ted, who had no conscience, grinned and nodded. "What are you all up to?" she asked, which made us laugh harder, as we imagined actually telling her. Her smile now included us all, and she laid her rare approval on us, on Ted lounging in the doorway, grinning, Joan and Kate rolling goofily on the beds, me holding my stomach on the floor, on all of us as we had frozen in our poses, miming the disgusted response of a poodle to the offer of her husband.

I arrived in Southampton around noon that Tuesday. I had told Mother I'd be there before lunch, but unless I arrived early she'd go out. Later she'd tell me I had said I was coming after lunch.

The house is made of whitewashed brick. It was built in the thirties, on part of a bigger property that had been split up. Like all Southampton houses it has a luscious velvet lawn, and those dense hedges. There are a few perfunctory flower beds, but Mother doesn't like gardening herself. She has Johnny Rubetti put in the garden for her, and every year he plants the world's most boring display of yellow, pink, and orange—dahlias, marigolds, and zinnias.

Mother was in the summer room, at the back of the house. The room was originally an open porch, then it was screened in, and now it is glassed in. It's meant to feel like part of the garden, so it's furnished with uncomfortable garden furniture, things that could, though they won't, be rained on. There are rattan sofas with flowered plastic-covered cushions and big porcelain elephants with flattened backs as end tables, and on the brick floor are woven straw rugs. When Joan first saw it she asked Mother, "Why don't you get some plaster gnomes, too?"

Mother was sitting in the comfortable chair, talking on the telephone. I waved, and she blinked at me in a friendly way, but went on talking. I went to the window and looked out. Johnny had been at work: there were the zinnias, starting up. The lawn was very lush, a deep, dense green like a mat, and that brilliant electric color made me think of our old house on the beach. We used to spend all our summers here in Southampton. Our house was huge: gray shingled, with white trim, and its roofs were thick with gables and dormers and clusters of brick chimneys. At the back of the house there was a lawn, and in the front there was the wide white beach, and beyond that there was the wide gray ocean, and beyond that there was Spain.

We children slept on the top floor, and all our windows looked out on the ocean. The rooms were small, with sloping eaves and rickety white-painted furniture: we loved them. The floors were painted a shiny gray, the white curtains blew in and out of the windows, and the air in our bedrooms at night was full of salt and freedom. Alone up there we were in our own country; we knocked messages on the walls, we had water fights, we slept in each other's rooms. No one knew what we did, only the maids came up there.

If we felt, during the winters in New York, as though we were members of the Underground, violent subversives whose activities were secret, we felt during the summers as though the liberation had come. In that wild salt air, the wind off the sea blew our tangled hair back off our faces as we rode our bikes up and down those narrow lanes, to the beach club, to the tennis club, to our friends' houses. We had our bikes, we had our friends, the days were long, and Harry came out only on the weekends. There were no rules that we cared about: don't put your wet bathing suits on the bed, be in by six or call. We had never heard of drugs, and the wickedest things we ever did were watching the boys smoke behind the beach club house, playing strip poker in whoever's house had no parents in it on rainy days. Sometimes we took surreptitious snorts out of someone's bottle at a beach party: a disgusting mixture of everything in someone's liquor cabinet, so that no one bottle would be diminished.

It wasn't so much what we did but the spirit in which we did it. In New York we had to obey Harry if he made one of his petulant announcements, but in Southampton we barely looked at him. We walked past him to say good night to Mother as though his chair were empty.

"Who's that girl won the junior tennis tournament?" Harry asked us. While he was still talking, still in the middle of his sentence, Joan turned and asked Kate a question in a low voice, which neatly removed them both from general conversation. This left me and Ted, neither of whom played tennis. This, plus the fact that I was five years younger than the girl (whose name I knew perfectly well), absolved me from answering. Ted looked intently into the middle distance, as though he were trying to remember the girl's name. Harry waited, watching us all, for a response. "Know who I mean?" he continued, "blond, kind of a cute girl? Think she's Jewish. Pretty sure she's Jewish. She go to the beach club or not?" At this point Joan and Kate very quietly asked my mother something, politely not interrupting Harry's conversation with the rest of us. I discovered a truly interesting bite on my leg. Ted continued to look deeply into the middle distance; if pressed by Harry now he would slowly shake his head, as if to show a respectful ignorance of the entire issue. Harry never acted snubbed, and he would finally turn his questioning to my mother. "Think she is. Think the whole family is," as though this were some sort of remarkable deductive leap. "Got to ask Bobby Woodward what's going on down here."

Mother ignored it all, Harry's efforts and our own rudeness, her blond hair smoothed back from her forehead in the velvet ribbon that picked up a color from her flowered linen dress. She had so many of those velvet ribbons, in so many beautiful colors; they lay in a neat jewel-like coil in the top drawer of her dressing table. No matter what dress she wore, one of her ribbons was the right color.

The summer that I was fourteen the others were away. Joan and Kate had gotten jobs on the Cape, and Ted was traveling in Europe. I missed them, especially Joan. It was not hard for me to keep up the glass wall that we had erected between ourselves and Harry, but, alone, it was more obvious that I was doing it. When Harry asked, "Where are you going tonight?" and looked directly at me, there was little I could do but respond. I delayed, of course. I took as long as I could to chew my food, and then I took a drink of milk, as though I could not possibly answer a question without a rinsed and perfectly empty mouth. Answering Harry, I looked ingenuously at Mother, as though the question were hers.

"The dance at the beach club," I said.

"Who with?" asked my mother.

"Everyone," I said, "we're all going."

"In whose car, though?" persisted Harry.

"Whose car?" I asked, frowning, as though it were not quite clear what he meant.

"Who is driving you to the club, and who is driving you back?" asked Harry.

"Oh, *driving*," I said innocently, as though I had thought

he had meant some other, vastly similar, activity. "I don't really know. Someone is picking me up. I'll get a ride back."

Harry looked at my mother, leaning forward in his chair, his gray eyebrows raised.

"Don't be in too late," Mother said warningly.

"Oh, I won't be," I said, with conviction. "It's just a dance."

They were never up when I got home. Every night of the year, after dinner, Mother and Harry each took another glass of Scotch, went into the library, and sat down at the backgammon table, where Harry believed he always won. At eleven o'clock Harry looked at his watch and said, "Time, gentlemen," and my mother said, "Well, it's a good thing. I'm about ready for the sandman myself," and they went up. We came home whenever we wanted.

After the dance some of us went down to the beach, where there was a fire. I got home around one-thirty. My ride dropped me off on the road, so the car wouldn't wake up Mother, and I walked up the driveway toward the house. It was a soft, bright night, with high clouds moving fast under a swollen white moon. I couldn't see it, but I could feel the presence, beyond the house, of the wide empty beach, and I could hear the long rolling waves, with their sleepy endless rhythm: skirling crash, and pause. In the moonlight the slate roof shone, and the chimneys were black: the house looked wonderful, like a castle full of secrets.

The house was usually dark except for a light in the back hall, by the kitchen, and I would go up the back stairs to my room. But that night the back hall was dark, and there was a light in the front hall and one in the library. I wondered if Harry and Mother were still playing backgammon, or if they had simply forgotten to turn off the light. I stepped into the front hall, pulling the door quietly behind me so it wouldn't slam. The living room was dark. I could see reflected gleams from polished things—mirrors, mahogany, porcelain. There was no sound, but I had the feeling someone was in the library, and I didn't want to go and see who it was. I started quietly toward the stairs, and had set my foot on the bottom step when I heard my name.

"Susannah?" I didn't want to break the late-night silence myself, so I went to the door and looked in at him.

"I'm home," I said.

Harry was sitting in the wing chair by the fireplace. The backgammon board was still out on the table, and there was a bottle of Scotch and his glass. He'd been smoking cigars, and the air was dense and fumy. He leaned back in his chair and folded his legs, in their pink trousers, at the ankle.

"Well," he said, smiling a little. "Home a bit late, aren't you?"

"No," I said. I didn't know what time it was, but I wasn't going to begin with an admission.

"I think so," said Harry, gleefully, "I think so." He waved his hand at me. "Come in and let's talk this over. I think your mother wouldn't like this, your coming in at this hour."

I wasn't crazy to have Mother hear what time I'd come back, so I moved in and stood in front of the cold fireplace. Harry was wearing an ascot tie, and it had come apart. The knot was still tight at his neck, but the flowing part was rucked up and hunched to one side, and his thick neck was exposed. I had never seen Harry's clothes messy before.

"I don't think your mother ought to hear about this," Harry said in a raspy whisper. His voice was blurry with Scotch. "What do you think?" He put his drink down carefully and put his elbows on the arms of his chair, steepling his hands and cocking his head at me. I didn't say anything.

"What do you think, Susannah? Do you think your

mother should know what time you came in tonight?" He made a show of pulling up his sleeve to look at his watch. "Quarter of two! Quarter of two in the morning!" He looked up at me. "Do you think she'd be glad to hear that?"

I stood in front of the cold fireplace, my hands crossed over my stomach.

"I'll tell you what," he said, leaning forward and putting his hand out. "Let's make a deal." He gave me a big glassy smile. "A deal? Okay?" I waited. "We won't either of us tell her." He held out his hand to shake, so I put mine out. He took hold of it in his big, puffy one as though he were shaking it, and at once put his other hand over the back of it. My poor fingers were trapped between those swollen cushions of flesh, these old damp pads moving slowly back and forth on my skin.

"I think we could keep a little secret from your mother, don't you, Susannah?" Harry was smiling at me now, the skin around his sunken eyes dense and white and grainy, like a lizard's throat. "Come sit down next to me, Susannah," he said, pulling me off balance, partly onto his lap. "We can be better friends than we have been. We can keep a secret, can't we." His smile was getting broader, it was quite friendly, and I half fell against his thin old legs in their soft cotton pants.

Falling into the chair against him, I struggled, but half-heartedly. I was used to his clean pink skin: I had had to kiss Harry good night since I was a baby. I'd been enfolded by his sagging arms before, I was used to the smell of him. Part of me was ready to fall against him again, unwillingly but dutifully, just the way I did saying good night, as though it were right. And I might have stayed there, I think, out of obedient habit, if he had kissed me the way I was used to, the way he always had. Instead, Harry put his hand on my thigh, my poor young thigh, under my wraparound Madras skirt, and he slid his damp, soft flesh up my leg. His breathing had changed, and he was still smiling but his eyes looked glazed. I was still off-balance, trying to pull myself back, sitting half on the arm of the chair and half on his lap. I could see his face, his neck starting to swell and turn red, and his eyes looking boiled. My poor leg, my poor, private adolescent thigh that didn't at all need touching, was aching, flaming with mortification. Then I struggled in earnest, writhing like a crazy-woman, at the thought of his moist old flesh, the secret horror that must be hidden in those soft cotton pants. When I got my balance, and struggled back onto the arm of the chair, I pushed his hand away as if it were made of poison, as if it would make blisters, as though it were a black spider creeping up my skin. I tried to get up, and he grabbed my hand and tried to pull me down again, thrusting out his lips—his lips!—as though the sight of them would change my mind, and I would soften, and lean over, and put my own on those bloated, liver-colored things.

But I had turned crazy. I felt as though I were wrestling with an octopus, soft, slimy, and underwater: I couldn't breathe. Wrestling, we knocked the lamp over, and when it crashed I fled. I left Harry in the dark library, with the smashed lamp on the floor, and I ran out into the hall. Up on the first landing I stopped, to listen. I heard myself, all my blood vessels open and roaring, my heart thundering along like a locomotive, but no noise from Harry, and no crackling of an electrical fire. I hoped he was dead. I hoped he would have a heart attack there alone in the stinking, disordered library. I took off my shoes and went on up to the third floor where I was safe. I slept in Joan's room, with the door locked.

In the morning I came down very late to breakfast, to

make sure I wouldn't see Harry. My mother was sitting alone at the glass-topped table. She was wearing a cotton shift printed with soft collapsing roses. It had modest slits up the sides, and little bows at the tops of them. Her shoes were rose colored, and so was her hair ribbon. She looked up at me briefly and down again at her breakfast on the pink linen mat in front of her.

"Good morning," she said, "Did you have a nice time at the dance?"

"Yes," I said. The breakfast room looked right out onto the ocean. There was an angry swell that morning, and the water heaved itself mutinously up on the beach.

"I gather you saw Harry when you got home," my mother said. She was spooning a boiled egg from an eggcup with sprigs of flowers all over it. She was concentrating hard, scooping out the rubbery white with a little egg spoon.

"Mmhmm," I said.

"I gather he wasn't very well," Mother said. Her mouth was turned down at the corners with what looked like disgust but was really concentration, as she scraped the insides of the shell with her spoon. "I gather you had a difficult time." She looked at me but I didn't say anything. "If he stays up late he gets very tired, and sometimes someone has to help him out."

I poured Cheerios into my flower-sprigged bowl, and covered them with cream. I ate them slowly, concentrating on the dry, grainy crunch, saying nothing. When I was finished I stood up. "I'm going to Elaine's," I said. Elaine was, of all my friends, my mother's least favorite. Mother always found a reason for me not to go to her house. That morning she nodded without looking up, the corners of her mouth still fastidiously turned down, and said, "Be back by lunch or call."

A *Glimpse of Scarlet*

*   *   *

My mother was wearing a flowered linen dress that morning, and her hair ribbon matched the tulips. When she put down the telephone, I started toward her chair to kiss her hello. Our kisses aren't much. There is no hugging, in fact there is not much contact at all. We take each other by the upper arms, lightly but firmly, as much to hold ourselves clear as to pull ourselves together. Then we place cheek against cheek, and we kiss the air. Still, I like these embraces. I like holding Mother's thin, cool body in my arms, just for a moment, smelling her soft skin. I know it's only a symbol, but it's a symbol of something I like. Sometimes I think I will tell her that, that I like kissing her. Sometimes I think I will take her into my arms and hold her, hug her like a child.

I leaned over to kiss my mother. I could smell her faint perfume as I bent over, but instead of reaching her cheek up toward mine she turned it away from me and held up her hand.

"I've stopped kissing people," she announced.

But it was too late. I couldn't stop myself, I was leaning over, with my hands out for her shoulders. Without them to brace myself I fell forward, onto my mother, in her chair. To my horror, I collapsed on top of her, struggling not to, struggling not to fall onto her thin old legs, her frail body, but finding myself in a ghastly moment of writhing face-to-face embrace. It was terrible. We were touching everywhere, breast, shoulder, rib cage, hands, our arms pushing each other frantically away, and my face brushed against hers anyway, horribly, as she had just asked me not to do. I pulled myself away from her as though I were burning her—I hadn't meant to force myself on my poor mother—and I stood up, my face flaming, mortified.

"Good heavens," I said inanely, a phrase I never use. "Are you all right? I didn't mean to fall on top of you."

My mother looked disgruntled and disordered, and she put herself back together, smoothing her skirt and patting her hair. "I'm fine," she said severely.

I moved away from her. "So you don't kiss *anyone?*" I asked, trying to sound casual and amused.

"No," Mother said, lighting a cigarette. "I've never liked it. Harry's dead, and I don't have to kiss anyone now. I don't have to and so I don't. My time for kissing is over." Mother settled back in her chair and crossed her narrow brown legs.

"So that's that," I said, smiling, but she wouldn't smile back.

"That's that." She took a long drag on her cigarette in its filtered holder.

It sounded so final. I couldn't think of anything to say, and I couldn't think of what to do with my hands. I felt off-balance and humiliated, and as I stood there, to my horror I felt my eyes begin to sting, the inside of my nose draw tight. I shook my head, but I could not keep it from happening: I began to cry in front of my mother, which was something I had never done. Out of shame I turned my face away.

I stood with my back to her, with my hands covering my face, my shoulders shaking, and I wept and wept and wept: a grown woman. My mother sat in the chair behind me and smoked. I heard her inhale. If she were to say anything I knew it would be, "Crying never helped." I hoped that she would say nothing, rather than that, and she did.

As I wept I thought of the things I had planned, sometime, to tell her. I had always thought that sometime we would sit down together, at peace, and she would lay on me her rare favor, and we would talk. I would tell her everything:

27

about Harry, about my life, about how it has been for John and me, and the troubles we've had with Amanda, and the times I have thought of divorce and despair. I had thought that this would happen, and now I could see that it would not.

There were things I had wanted to ask her, too: what it was like for her, what it was like being married to my charming, impossible father, and how it was to marry instead someone with money, who could help her bring up her children.

Her four children, who laughed at her husband behind her back, who cut her cruelly out of their lives, who made their own secret and vivid lives up without her, who frightened her so that she did not dare look at them, so that she did not dare ask them for anything, for fear they would deny it. And how it would be for her now, alone, in her small house with the velvet lawn, with her thin, dry, sleek legs, her beautiful velvet hair ribbons and her Cavalier King Charles spaniel, now that she has given up kissing people.

LAYERING

&

We are in the back yard, on the lawn. It is August, and very hot. It is hard to move, and hard to think of a reason to. Yesterday my stepson, who is twelve years younger than me, came in to the room where I was sketching. He is staying alone with us for the month of August, a first. He did not look at what I was doing, he never does. He seems to feel that the things I do are terribly private. He kept his eyes away from my paper—I was doing a sketch of a weed I had pulled up from the garden, roots, dirt, and all—and asked me where he could get a haircut. Jonathan, his father, gets his cut in the city now, so I don't know any good places nearby. There is a terrible little dive in the village, I tell him, with a fly-specked barber pole on the front porch, and girlie calendars on the wall. I walk past it on the opposite side of the street, it gives me the creeps.

Frank asks me if I will cut his hair. I cut his hair when he was nine years old, a small boy. He hated the sight of himself afterward, and his mother called up Jonathan and told him I was presumptuous. That was eight years ago, and Frank is now taller than I am, with a devotion to sun rays and his track team. He has wide shoulders and narrow hips and long legs and he is very, very tanned. He goes running in the evenings, and when he returns my dog starts out across the lawn, thinking those rapid, steady footsteps might belong to a cat burglar, or a second-story man. Halfway across the lawn she begins to wag her tail and then sits down and yawns, pretending that she knew all along that the footsteps belonged to Frank, who loves her.

I told Frank I would cut his hair, but later. I could not have sounded eager, because when we went into the village in the afternoon he walked over to the dive to make an appointment with the calendar collector, but it was shut.

We were on our own for most of the week. Jonathan travels a lot. Frank went to his tutoring in the mornings, and I sketched. After lunch we went up to play tennis on the red clay court up in the woods. Each day we promise that next time we'll really work on it. We have to keep propping up the posts that hold up the net, and the net itself is full of holes. The surface is soft, and there are pine needles all over it, which makes for exciting bounces. Frank's serve can tunnel right under my feet, when it goes in, but he's erratic, and I still beat him 6-1. Most of his shots go out, but he's faster and stronger than I am, and he gets to everything. I just send the ball back until he gets impatient, tries for a winner, and hits it into the net. It won't be too much longer that I can beat him.

After we played tennis that day we walked back to the house through the pine woods. It was high midday, and most of the insects were quiet. There were a lot of crows walking around in the field, having a meeting. My dog spends most of her time disrupting their meetings, she is nearly a professional at this, but this time she was down by the house in the shade, her raspberry tongue hanging out.

We went down and lay on the back lawn, underneath the ash tree. Even the lawn gave off heat, even the grass was hot. My dog came over and lay down next to me. I rubbed her nose and she lost control. She rolled over onto her back and opened her mouth like a crocodile, and showed the whites of her eyes.

"You are wacko, Beedle," Frank said, digging his knuckles into his eyes. Beedle flipped herself over toward him and wagged her tail, on her back. Her tongue fell out sideways on the grass.

"Where's Dad?'" asked Frank.

"Houston," I said.

"When's he coming home?"

"Tomorrow or Thursday."

I closed my eyes and began to go to sleep. There were cicadas in the trees all around us. It was past midsummer, all right, we were heading into fall. One of the trees along the fence, a swamp maple, was showing yellowy-orange. I lay without moving, my head toward my shoulder, my legs crossed at the ankles.

"So, are you going to cut my hair?" Frank asked.

I was asleep, and reluctant. I opened my eyes and closed them again. "Sure," I said. We listened to the cicadas. I started to go back to sleep.

"Now?" asked Frank.

"Sure," I said.

Frank brought out an old wicker armchair and a comb, and I got out the scissors. I started cutting. I don't know why I first thought I could cut hair—no one ever taught me—but I've been doing it ever since boarding school. I have always cut my own. By now, if I'm not particularly good at it, at least I know what I can do. Men's haircuts are always trims. You just shorten everything. If it's layers, you shorten each layer. If it's a bowl cut, you get a smaller bowl. Frank's hair was very thick, and had lots of layers. I started out at the top, using the comb to pull up a clump and let it fall. I thought this looked very professional, though I don't know why barbers do it. In any case Frank had no mirror and couldn't see I was doing it so I stopped and began snipping. My dog came over and leaned against my leg.

"Hi, Beedle," I said. I stopped and rubbed her.

Frank sat very straight. He was wearing only a pair of red basketball shorts, and he was perfectly tanned, all over his shoulders and his arms and his legs. His legs were crossed at the ankle, like a good child.

"You know how to do this, don't you?" he asked.

"Hey," I said, "what kind of question is that?" Snip, I went, snip. I wondered if I were cutting it too short. "Just tell me how you want it, man." Sometimes Frank and I talk the way we think black people talk, sometimes it's other ethnic groups. I don't know why we do this.

Frank put his hands back, pulling at his hair. "I want it pretty short over the ears," he said, pulling at it. I started out on the right side, above the ear. His ear was perfectly brown, like the rest of him. Frank had his ear pierced in the spring, and his girlfriend gave him a diamond stud. He is very good-looking, but he has a round, honest face, with raised eyebrows, and that diamond stud looks out of place, as though he were trying to pass for a cad.

I pulled the hair away from his ear and began to cut it. Snip, I went, snip. I kept brushing at his ear. It was very soft: ears are always soft. No one has tough ears. I tried to keep my fingertips away from Frank's ear, but they kept brushing at it. I pulled out big hanks of hair from the top and the side with the comb, and gave good professional swipes to them, straight-edge cuts. Then I had to do the back of his neck. Frank bowed his head, his back still very straight. There were bits of clipped hair on his shoulders, a lot of little brown hairs littering those straight, perfectly tanned shoulders. It was very hot, and the hair was sticking to his skin. It was so hot we were both sweating, very lightly, but everywhere. Everywhere there was any touch on our skins at all the skin responded by glistening and turning moist. So all those hairs stayed on Frank's tanned shoulders.

Frank and I have always gotten along, it's his younger sister I fight with. Jonathan wouldn't have dreamed of leaving me alone with her. Once, though, I made Frank cry. He dropped all three plates of spaghetti he was carrying, after assuring me everything would be fine. I yelled at him, never imagining that he would cry: he had been so certain of things the moment before. I felt bad for weeks. He was nine years old, and was kind to me when I apologized.

One of the cats came and jumped into Frank's lap. They don't ever stop to think if you want a cat in your lap, cats just jump in. Frank laughed and started to stroke him. "Did you think I was lonely?" he asked the cat, "did you think I was missing a cat? It's too hot to have a cat in your lap, didn't you know that?"

The cat lifted his head and closed his eyes. He knew better than to listen. This is a messy blond cat who sheds, and hairs come off with every stroke. Now they floated aimlessly in the heavy air, and Frank's legs began to have little blond wisps on them.

Sometimes I cut Jonathan's hair, too. Every time I touch his hair I stroke his head, so that it is a nice, long doting session. I am allowed to touch his ears, and follow them around the curve and blow into them to clear them of the clipped hair. Jonathan lifts up one shoulder to ward me off: I'm supposed to be just cutting his hair.

"No degenerate behavior," he says, but he loves it.

I had not been looking forward to spending August with Frank: I thought he was going to be a belligerent teenager, playing the radio loudly all over the house and using the telephone all the time and complaining about everything. Wrong. All he's been is nice, carrying things in from the car without being asked and helping with the animals and cutting the lawn without griping and being tutored in the mornings and studying in the evenings (which is why he's with us for this month). He does everything without griping, with real grace, in fact, and I began to feel very silly, all my preparations for war, all my ultimatums and decrees, how I would quell him if Jonathan were away and there was an uprising. Instead I got this calm, mild, good-natured kid. I was ashamed of myself. I'd snapped at him in the beginning, just to open hostilities. "*Don't* bounce that ball in the kitchen," I had said, sounding like someone just before they grab the axe.

Frank shook his head and took the ball outside. "Don't get so crazy," he said.

In the back I tried to follow the curve of his head. That's the way it was layered, and I trimmed each layer. Frank put his hand back and felt it. "*There*," he said, "and *there*. Isn't it too long?"

"Ah'll cut it fo' you," I said, imitating someone from Mississippi, "Ah just doan' want to cut it too short." I was afraid of that, afraid that he would hate what I had done to him.

I clipped along the back of his neck. Frank tucked his chin in and dropped his head as though he were in church, a young penitent. The hair along the back of his neck was soft and fuzzy, a different texture from the rest. It was golden brown, and the skin just underneath it was not tanned, but pale and very soft. Each time I took a clump of hair, my fingers rubbed against the back of Frank's neck.

"What are those insects?" Frank asked.

"Katydids."

"But what's their real name?"

"I don't know how to pronounce it. Keep your head down." I pushed gently at his head.

"You know when I went into the city last week?" Frank's voice was a little choked, from keeping his head bent down so far. "I was walking along Park Avenue and I saw a car parked in front of a building, all loaded up with suitcases and things, a station wagon. There was a man getting out of it, and a woman, and there were two kids in the doorway of the building. I don't know what made me think of it, but all of a sudden I thought she's not their mother. I kept watching them, even after I'd passed them on the sidewalk I kept turning back to look at them."

I kept on clipping Frank's hair.

"What did she do?" I asked.

"She just waited by the car. The man went over to the children and brought them back to the car."

"And did she kiss them?"

"I don't know," said Frank, "by then I was too far away. But I kept thinking how strange it must be for her, to be in the middle of someone else's family."

"It must be strange for the kids," I said. Frank uncrossed his feet, then he crossed them again, left over right this time. "Well," he said.

"It makes me crazy sometimes," I said. "I take it out on you. But it isn't you." I have never told Frank that I love him.

35

"It's okay," Frank said, pushing his hair away from his forehead. "I mean, you're fine." He cleared his throat. He was trying to put me at ease.

I had gotten to the front. "Do you have a part?" I asked.

"Do I have a part?" Frank was outraged, disgusted with me. "Je-sus. How long have you known me? I have *always* had a part."

"Well, part it, then," I said, clicking my scissors in the air as though I had other customers waiting. He parted it, and I began again: snip.

"You're done," I said at the end.

"Would you brush the hair off my shoulders?"

I began to brush the hair off Frank's shoulders. He sat perfectly still. The sweat, that fine film of moisture, kept the hairs sticky and heavy. They moved a little bit when I brushed them, but they didn't fly lightly into the air. The palms of my hands, the tips of my fingers were damp, too. It was terribly hot. The skin I was brushing was no kin to me. His flesh was from another woman's body, a woman who still will not speak my name. Frank's shoulders are perfectly tanned and smooth, he is the youngest of young men, with not a mark on him. I brushed at him and brushed at him, and began to laugh.

"Mon, you look a wocko mon," I said, talking like Bimini. "You look like a crazy mon. You grow de brown hair on de head, de brown hair on de back, de yellow hair on de legs." I began to sing "Yellow Hair," to the tune of "Yellow Bird."

"Yeah, well, who's wacko around here," Frank said. He stood up, brushing at himself, all around the back of his neck. He is five inches taller than me now. I stooped down and started petting the cat, who had been deposited on the lawn. The dog pressed against my leg, lobbying for more attention. Frank went into the house for a mirror. I crouched next to the animals, feeling strange. My dog rolled heavily onto her side, and lifted her front paw, tilting her chin to one side.

Frank came out of the back door, letting the screen slam behind him. He had my silver-backed hand mirror stuck in the top of his shorts, like a gun.

"Well?" I asked.

"Good," he said, "but I want the back shorter. I want it to look like Dad's."

"Okay," I said, "get back in the chair."

Again I bent over his hot back, sweeping each wisp of golden-brown, downy neck hair very carefully into a little clump, and carefully, very carefully, bringing the scissors alongside them, evenly, so that the cut would be straight, and so that the points would not prick Frank's skin. I was trying not to touch Frank's damp, innocent skin.

A GLIMPSE OF SCARLET

❧

The week before Labor Day is the quietest of the year in New York. Everyone is somewhere else, holding on to the last loose days of summer, the last glimmer of freedom. In the city, it's like being on the bottom of a lake: a deep, dreaming moment. The air is hushed and motionless, sounds are close and intimate, the plants and trees are huge and luxuriant from the summer in the solar greenhouse of the city.

There was a teachers' meeting at school that week, so I was in town, and Guy was at work, so he was there. The meeting was over around four-thirty, and I walked home across town. Those shady, quiet streets in the East Seventies were deserted. The brownstones had been closed up since June.

I started up the block between Third and Lexington. There were young sycamore trees in neat planted squares along the sidewalk. Wisteria and trumpet vines hung in swooping tangles across the houses, and impatiens plants stood in damp jungles around the tree trunks. Everything was hot and lush and quiet. I walked slowly. It was strange, being in the city like that. The boys were still out in the country, staying with friends. With no children, no friends there I felt adrift, as though I were alone in a foreign city. Anything might happen, in that heat and silence.

One of the front doors opened ahead of me, and a man stepped out onto the stoop. His shoulders were hunched and protective, and he moved gently, as though he were trying to be invisible. He did not look around, he was afraid of catching an eye. It was the urgency of this, his not wanting to be seen, that caught my attention. He was rigid with it. He turned to close the door, and as he did so he looked back at someone just inside. I caught a glimpse of something red, a violent color, vivid and hot. It was a sleeve, a scarf—I couldn't see—but the man in his rumpled gray suit leaned in toward it, and was taken in a kiss. That was clear, the way he leaned in, the way his body longed inward.

The kiss went on and on. I wondered if he would give in to it, and step back inside the door and close it behind him again, but he pulled himself away in the end. It was quarter to five, and finally he pulled himself back, and closed the door and stepped quietly down the stone steps. The door opened again, just for a moment. She didn't want to let him go. There was no light on inside, the doorway was dark, but again I saw a glimmer of scarlet. The man didn't risk his invisibility again, though, he didn't look back. He went down the steps quickly, his eyes lowered. But I was staring, and as he came past me I caught his eye—he didn't want me to! I was transfixed. It was so clear what he had come from.

What boldness, lying there in her husband's house, the shades drawn against the August afternoon, lying amid the silence of her marriage, surrounded by her life with someone else, everything overshadowed by the fact of her husband. Her husband: no matter where on earth he was definitely, absolutely, unalterably known to be that afternoon, there was the possibility, simple and likely, that he would unexpectedly put his key into his own front door at any moment. While the two of them whispered upstairs, on those musky sheets, her husband might easily be stepping across the doorstep into the front hall of his own house, setting down his briefcase, turning over the letters on the hall table before he put his foot on the bottom step of the stairs.

How brave, how desperate, how admirable of this man, I thought. All that risk, the guilt, the danger, balanced against something so rich, so sumptuous, so imperative that he had no choice but to risk it all. He could see that I knew what he had come from. He was ordinary looking, thin, with narrow shoulders, a lined face and vanishing hair, a small round chin. To look at him you would have seen nothing extraordinary—but I knew the current he was helpless in, I knew the strength of it. As I met his eyes he looked partly guilty, partly defiant. It was clear that he had no choice. He turned away, but I watched him, filled with admiration. He walked down the street past me, carrying his briefcase, shrugging his shoulders into his suit, stretching his chin, settling himself into anyone else. I looked back at the house he had come from, but there was nothing. She had gone. She was padding barefoot back up the stairs to the room they had used: a child's, or the back guest bedroom. She was going to make the bed up clean, but first she might, for a moment, sink into it again, gathering up the sheets and pressing her face against them, closing her eyes into all that pleasure.

Our doorman waits intently behind the big glass doors of our building, scanning the street. When he sees one of us he springs to life, hauling on the heavy door before you can touch it. That afternoon he pulled it smoothly open before me, nodding.

"Good afternoon, Mrs. Cunningham," he said briskly, "Mr. Rosen," he added, to the man coming in behind me. Mr. Rosen and I got into the elevator—he lives above us— and I thought: I could never have an affair here. We'd have to meet somewhere else. I was still in the spell of that empty street, the humid air, that man leaning inside for a moment and being taken in a kiss. The extremity, the secrecy, and the great violence of the pleasure.

Our apartment was dim and quiet. No one would be home for hours. The tall French doors at the end of the living room were luminous shapes against the long summer evening. I was alone in the shadowy rooms. The bedrooms upstairs were empty. I stepped into the front hall quietly, making no sound on the parquet. I moved up the dim staircase toward our bedroom as though there were a man behind me, silent, urgent, his breath held, as mine was, as though we had no choice.

Don't misunderstand me: I don't want an affair. I had one during my first marriage. That current takes you over the falls, there's no changing your mind once you've started. You deceive yourself at first: you pretend that what you want is something quite innocent. When you can no longer pretend that, you pretend that it is what you deserve, and that no one will be hurt. When you can no longer pretend that, it is too late to pretend anything at all: there you are, with the scarlet letter on your forehead, and all around you in broken pieces on the ground. It's not what I want. Guy and I have been married now for seven years, and that's what I want. But I see that between us all the violence has gone, all the urgency dissolved—as it should, as it must, in seven years. And sometimes, when I suddenly see it in someone else's life, it comes back to me, that lovely, voluptuous thrill. The extremity, the secrecy, and the great violence of the pleasure.

It was about three weeks after school started that Alden called me there. I never get calls at school, for one thing, and for another I haven't heard from Alden in nearly ten years, even though he lives ten or twelve blocks away. Our lives changed absolutely away from each other, as they had to. I'm a tutor in remedial reading. Ordinarily I'm busy every period, but that day Jamie Wainwright was home sick, so at ten o'clock I was sitting on the grubby chintz sofa in the teachers' lounge and listening to Helen Chisholm tell me about her fertility problems. Helen's class—first grade—was in the music room, so we had the whole forty minutes to discuss her new doctor.

"He wants to send me to a place in Virginia," Helen said. "You go there for two weeks and you come back pregnant."

"Virginia?" I said. "That's convenient."

Helen laughed and shrugged. She is round-faced, with a neat round cap of hair, and round-rimmed glasses. She looks like one of those figures that beginners can draw, using only circles.

"Oh, it's very convenient. Malcolm is thrilled. The whole *business* is convenient, let me tell you. Malcolm has to drop off a new sample each time I switch doctors. Then he has to produce a new sample every month. He says he's got the fastest hands in the East."

"Poor Malcolm," I said, thinking of him trudging around with a screw-top jar. I also felt faintly smug, that I had managed two boys without any effort at all. Granted, it had been the wrong marriage, but there they were, twelve and fourteen, sane and healthy.

When the telephone buzzed I picked it up, expecting to take a message for someone else.

"Lisa?"

A voice you've known like that is a star bursting inside you, whether you want it or not.

"Hello," I said.

"What's up?" Alden's voice was as close, as casual as though we'd spent the night together. I began to laugh. I was frightened.

"Well," I said, "not much."

"Want to have lunch?"

"Lunch?" I said.

"I've been thinking about you," Alden said.

"You have?" I wanted to get off the phone.

"I've been wondering how you were."

"Well, I'm fine," I said. But I couldn't pretend that there was any distance between us, I couldn't pretend that Alden didn't know exactly who I was.

"Oh, you are," he said, "gee, that's great." He began to laugh at my dopey answer, and I couldn't help it, I began to laugh too, as though we were close friends, as though ten years hadn't ground by between us.

"So," he said, "when are we going to have lunch?"

"I don't know," I said, "I'll call you."

"Great," he said. There was a silence. "Only you won't."

I looked at my fingernails. "I might not."

There was another pause. We listened for each other.

"Well, it's been good talking to you," Alden said finally, making it funny, and he started to laugh again. "Really great."

"Right," I said. I wondered what Helen was thinking.

"I saw you on the street the other day."

For some reason I thought at once of the day I saw the man coming out of the brownstone.

"You look great," Alden said, his voice serious. "You look spectacular."

There was a long silence. I look the way I look, and it's my business. Someone watching me on the street, making his own decisions about it—I didn't like it.

"Well," I said, "thank you."

Alden waited for a moment.

"Bye," he said.

"Bye," I answered, and we hung up.

My face was hot, my whole skin was anxious. Helen was watching me. I got up to make myself a cup of tea.

"Was that Guy?" she asked.

"Yes," I said, before I thought. I stood at the hot water machine, my back to her, slowly dipping my tea bag again and again, keeping my face turned away. I was afraid that she would see that my face was hot, that my system was running on Alarm, that I had told a flat-out lie.

"Well," Helen said, sipping from her mug, "so I guess I'm going to try this thing in Virginia. I feel like a brood mare, being shipped down for breeding."

"And what's the process? What do they do down there?" I asked, squeezing the tea bag around my spoon. I wanted to talk about anything but my phone conversation: my heart was still racing, as though I'd been caught stealing.

"It's in vitro," said Helen, "you know, you must have read about it." She sighed.

"In vitro," I said, carrying my mug back and sitting down across from her again. I thought of steel instruments entering your body, doing things they had no business

44

doing, I thought of shining glass dishes stirring with bits of life. "That sounds, I don't know, awfully extreme, doesn't it?"

"Extreme," Helen said, looking at me. She stirred her tea. "Have you ever thought about what it's like, not being able to have a baby?" I didn't say anything: I hadn't really. "It takes over every thought in your life. You look at every woman on the sidewalk to see if she's pregnant, and if she is you hate her. You turn your face away from her, you close your eyes as she walks past. There are friends of mine I can't see anymore, I don't even want to talk to them on the phone, because they have children." As she talked Helen began to cry. Tears ran down her cheeks into the corners of her mouth, and as they got close enough she licked them off. "Every month becomes a misery to you. Malcolm and I fight all the time, over stupid things, not over the fact that he's angry that I'm so angry, and I'm so angry you can't imagine it. Your whole life is consumed by it, and there's nothing you can do, nothing."

Helen took a Kleenex out of her pocket and put it over her nose, and then she covered her face with her hands.

"Oh, Helen," I said, "I'm so sorry."

She shook her head, and the two of us sat there in that sad, unpainted room, in silence. It was as though a tremor had run through the ground beneath us, reminding us that there was chaos below. I wanted to think things were governed by logic, but here we were: why was Helen grieving and empty instead of a mother? And I, why did I feel shaken and undone by Alden's call, as though I had come very close to something dangerous, why had I lied about it, as though I had done something wrong, when I had done nothing at all, when I didn't want to feel that way at all, when that wasn't what had happened at all?

*　　*　　*

Fixing dinner that night I was as nervous as a bird. Would I tell Guy about the phone call or not? My son Alex slid into the kitchen in his stockinged feet, his shirttails hanging over his baggy pants. He poured a huge glass of orange juice.

"I have late soccer practice tomorrow," he announced.

"Good," I said. I would definitely tell Guy. I'd wipe the slate clean. We don't keep things from each other. I took the lamb chops out of the refrigerator.

"Why good?" Alex asked. He licked the orange juice off around his mouth.

"I mean, not good," I said. But if I told Guy that Alden had called, he would think it was important, he would think I was warning him that something significant had happened. I began to wash the broccoli.

Alex drank a second glass of orange juice like a chicken, his mouth wide open and his chin pointing straight up into the air.

"Why *not* good?" he asked. He wadded up the paper bag the broccoli had come in and dropped it on the floor. He began kicking it from foot to foot.

"I don't mean that," I said. Where had I put the lamb chops? They had vanished. Maybe I was being cowardly, not telling. Certainly Guy would be angry if I told him. He'd see it as unfair, for one thing. He never does this kind of thing to me: Guy is as solid as a rock. And he knows who Alden is in my life. He sees Alden's figure outlined in red, DANGER stamped across it.

"What *do* you mean, then?" Alex asked cheerfully.

I stared at him. "I don't know what I mean," I said firmly. Alex grinned and tapped his head. He began sliding up and down past me in the narrow kitchen, making dazzling goals with the broccoli bag. I found the lamb chops in the refrigerator. Had I put them back, or had I imagined taking them out? And was I going to tell Guy or not?

He appeared in the doorway. Guy is tall and narrow, with very blond hair, nearly white, and a noble, beaky nose. He stretched his arms up and grabbed the top of the door frame. His jacket opened, showing his rumpled shirt. The light from overhead darkened the lines in his cheeks, and there were circles under his eyes.

"Phew," he said, "what a day." He came over to kiss me. He moved slowly.

"What happened?"

"Nothing. Tried to get in to see Kaplan."

"And?"

"Couldn't. I'll tell you: I can't wait to get away from here."

"To Portugal? Or you mean just this weekend?"

"Anywhere," Guy said, "either. Both. Just away."

There's something going wrong for Guy at his law firm. There's nothing I can do about it. I'd like to, I'd like to act like those mothers who come into school, fresh from the hairdresser, my high heels clicking on the long hallways. I'd like to make an appointment with the senior partner, and wave my finger at him behind the closed doors of his office. I'd like to make accusations: favoritism, perfidy, unfairness. I'd like to extract apologies for the past, and promises for the future.

I put my arms around him as hard as I could. Definitely, I wouldn't tell him about the phone call.

That weekend we were in the country. We have a small, unkempt house in Watermill, which is quiet. We have friends with big, kempt houses in Southampton, which is not. On Saturday night we went to a dinner party at a house that might as well have been at Sixty-eighth and Fifth, not on the outermost reaches of Long Island. The dining room had oxblood enameled walls, and over the sideboard was a mirror framed by a gilt serpent, his tail in his mouth. On either side of it were ormolu sconces, with orchids poised on them. The women were all in silk and real jewelry. As we came in to dinner, the candlesticks gleaming, the deep, rich walls enclosing us all, stern waiters in white coats ready to serve, strange men on either side of me, I thought of starting the skein of conversation, asking questions it might be interesting for these men to answer. I hate strange men, I thought, and looked around for Guy. But he was at another table; I heard his laugh again and again during the meal.

As soon as dinner was over I said good night and edged past the people in the *faux marbre* front hall. They were all kissing the air past one another's cheeks and telling lies about calls they would make, lunches they would share. I stepped out alone onto the big front porch. The great night sky expanded in a rush above me, the silence took hold of me, and the soft air came in off the water like perfume. I stood there taking deep breaths and trying to absorb the soft dark night, trying to splinter that dense, enameled evening.

When people came out behind me, I moved down onto the driveway to wait for Guy. He came out with a group of people. He was talking loudly; he'd had some wine.

"I'll call you, then," he said, looking at something in his hand. "We'll go to the Hard Rock Cafe." He was talking to a girl in a low-backed black dress. She had short blond hair, and seemed sleek and self-possessed. Guy looked at the crowd around him. "And if you see us having lunch," he said, to the world, "just pretend you don't." He laughed.

It was utterly unlike Guy. I walked across the driveway

and got into our car. On the way home, Guy told me what a good time he'd had. He'd sat next to a girl named Sylvia Patton, a writer who was very funny and very bright. And she had a lisp that Guy had noticed. He mentioned it several times. It seemed he had liked it.

At home I undressed and got into a nightgown: something I don't ordinarily wear. I got into bed and picked up my book. I began to read. Guy got into bed and reached for me. I didn't move.

"What's the matter?"

"Nothing." These are formalities.

"Come on," Guy said, pulling gently at me.

"I didn't like that joke about you having lunch with that girl."

Guy sighed. "Now, look," he said. "Sylvia knows the Algarve very well. We're just getting together so that she can tell me places for us to go."

I sat up in bed and stared at him. "Wait a minute," I said. "You're serious? You're really planning to go off and have lunch alone with this woman?"

"We haven't set a specific day for it, if that's what you mean," Guy said.

"Even now," I said, "even now you think this is all right? That you're going off to have lunch alone with this strange woman? At the Hard Rock Cafe?"

Guy sighed, as though I were a hysterical woman and he were a reasonable man. "The Hard Rock Cafe is a good place for us to go because they have big tables, so we can spread out the maps."

"No other reasons," I said. "It has no other connotations. I suppose you take your clients there all the time, so you can spread out your *briefs*."

Guy sighed again.

"And why do you have to have lunch with her to see the maps? They can't be sent through the mails? They're contraband maps?"

"You're trying to pick a fight," Guy said loftily.

"I can't *believe* you're saying that."

"Sylvia knows a lot about the place we're going," Guy said. "It will be more fun for us if I find out things for our trip."

"*Our* trip?" I said. "*I'm* not tagging along to the Algarve to see the places you and Adorable Lisp have picked out. Take her to the goddamned Algarve."

Guy turned on me. He became a lawyer. "Are you telling me," he said severely, "are you telling me that you *seriously* do not want to come on our trip to Portugal?"

"Yes," I said instantly.

I was so angry. And in the middle of it I was impressed by it, by the rage. Sometimes the connections between Guy and me seem like soft old ropes, turned slack and listless with age. This violence! I hadn't expected it.

"Well, you've set a precedent," I announced. "After the next dinner party, I may perfectly well come home giggling about the wonderful man I sat next to, and tell you we're going to have lunch next week, so he can give me the book we talked about."

Guy pulled the sheets up high under his arms and lay flat on his back. "You're making something of nothing," he said, staring straight up at the ceiling. "Good night." He closed his eyes.

I thought of something.

"If this is nothing," I said, "then why did you look around and say to everyone, 'If you see us having lunch, pretend you don't'?"

I saw Guy's eyes flicker open for a moment. He shut

them again at once, pulled the sheets up tighter and settled himself more firmly in bed, his chin stuck out high in the air like the prow of a ship. He wouldn't answer. It didn't matter. I had seen the flicker.

It was midnight. Guy lay there pretending to be asleep until he was. By then he had relaxed, and his lovely round shoulders were curved open against the sheets. His breathing had slowed and lengthened. I looked at him, at his elegant, bony shoulders, his smooth neck, his startling pale hair. I wanted to stroke his hair, but of course I didn't.

I lay and read the same page over and over until one-thirty. Then I turned out the light and lay pulsing in the dark. I could hear my heart pounding along. It was so loud in my ears that I wondered if it would wake Guy. I lay very still; he needed to sleep.

At four o'clock I thought of something else. Guy had had something in his hand, out in the parking lot. At this very moment, in the same room with his wife, Guy had a token of his meeting. It was in the room with me.

I got out of bed and moved quietly across the room. I tripped over a scrap basket, knocking it over. I could hear no noise: my heart was hammering like a demon carpenter. I reached the bureau and began touching the things on top of it. There was Guy's wallet. There were his cuff links, his silk handkerchief. No slip of paper. I went into the alcove and turned on the light. I found Guy's blazer and pants hanging in the closet. I went through the pockets. My heart was crashing still, racing: I wondered if I would know it if I were having a heart attack. There was nothing in the pockets. I went back into the bedroom and tripped over the scrap basket again. I found Guy's wallet and brought it into the bathroom. I opened it over the sink.

Guy's wallet is fat and smooth, made of soft, limp leather.

It bulges with important facts about Guy: his lawyerness, his citizenship, his fiscal responsibilities. I scrabbled inside it. Sylvia's note was tucked neatly into the first flap next to Guy's business cards, her name set tightly against his. *Sylvia Patton*, it said, and then her home number and her service. Holding it, I felt as though I were touching raw plutonium.

I tore the note crosswise, then lengthwise. I tore it into as many pieces as I could. I threw them violently into the toilet. They floated mildly down, and settled on the pale surface of the water. I pushed viciously at the lever. The water rose, the scraps swirled, everything sank. The water rose again, empty.

It was over; the note was gone.

I picked up Guy's wallet, and saw myself in the mirror. The greenish light flickered overhead. My pupils were huge and black, my shoulders were hunched against the late-night chill. I held someone else's wallet in my hands, like a thief. The house was silent, and the empty night spread out around me. I didn't like the way I looked.

My sense of outrage began to ebb. I began to wonder what I'd done. The bottom seemed to fall away beneath me: it was possible now that Guy had been right, that I was making something out of nothing. I felt as though I'd killed something.

Oh, there had been something. I had seen that flicker in Guy's eyes. But it was only a flicker. Just for one moment, standing under the great expanding night sky after dinner, the stars pulsing overhead, the wine pulsing within, Sylvia smiling at him and declaring her love for the place he'd chosen, he must have felt a moment of widening freedom, possibility, a glimpse of scarlet. Just as I had, my pulse clamoring at Alden's voice.

It was that moment I had destroyed, that brief freedom,

with all my wildness, all my rage. I had beaten it down, I had choked it utterly. And I was swept with shame, and with tenderness for my husband, lying there so warm and elegant in the next room, needing his sleep, needing his freedom.

But what could I do? What else could I have done?

SECOND CHANCES

It was raining when I woke up on Thanksgiving morning. Nick was just coming to life, stretching his arms out and making weird suppressed moans. I went in to Jessie's room to make sure she was up. The car was coming to take her to her father's house early, at seven-thirty.

Jessie was up, but barely. She was sitting on the edge of her bed in her scarlet long johns, her pillow in her lap. She is just thirteen, and has, in a bold stroke, cut off the luxuriant mane of her childhood. Her hair is now shorter than Nick's, and she looks like a trim little boy from the nineteen fifties.

"You're awake," I said, nearly whispering. Around us the house slept. She nodded, heavy-eyed. "The car will be here in half an hour."

"It's going to be so *boring* there," Jessie said.

"Maybe not," I said, pleased.

"Yes, it will," Jessie said bitterly. "We're going to the Wades', and everyone else there will be grown-ups or tiny children, and I'll have to stand around by myself for three thousand years."

"Well, at least you got to see Grandma and Grandpa," I

said. My parents had arrived the night before, especially to
see Jess.

"And I got to help you set the table, and polish the silver,
and make the centerpiece," Jessie said, and sighed. "Will you
save me some pie?"

The car arrived at twenty past. The driver was a new
one, a Chinese man who smiled and held a striped umbrella
over Jessie's head as they went out to the car. I stood in the
driveway, in the drizzle, in my bathrobe and floppy red
slippers, and Jessie and I waved at each other for as long as
we could, as the big car eased its way around the circle,
underneath the great standing willows, down the slope and
past the stone wall to the road. I was still waving when it
nosed between the stone pillars out onto the muddy road,
and still waving when it finally disappeared among the wet
black trees, taking with it all reason for Thanksgiving.

I went back inside to get dressed. The day, I supposed,
had begun. Nick was gone when I got to the bedroom, and
I stared at the big rumpled bed. I wanted to get back in it
and pull the covers over my head.

Jessie's father, Chad, gets her for alternate holidays. This
year he got her for Thanksgiving and I get her for Christmas.
When his secretary called about picking Jess up, I explained
about my parents being there on a Wednesday night to see
her. Could she leave on Thursday morning, I asked, instead
of Wednesday afternoon? She said she'd ask. She sounded
nervous. Chad called me right back, and the tone of his voice
made things clear from the start. We've been divorced for
eleven years, and you'd think—or at least I keep thinking—
that things will slowly wear smooth between us, that these
jagged edges will be worn away. This doesn't happen. His
rage at me is unabated, a fresh flower of fire each time.

"What is all this about Thanksgiving, Kate?" he asked,

furious. "It's my turn to have her, and that's that. Don't start trying to screw things up."

"I don't want to screw anything up," I said. "It's just that my parents will be here on Wednesday night, and she'd like to see them."

"You always do this," Chad said. "Lizzie will be wild when she hears what you're up to."

Lizzie is his wife. "Maybe I should talk to Lizzie directly," I said, "I'm sure she understands about grandparents."

"Lizzie doesn't want to talk to you," Chad said. "Lizzie hates your guts. She'd like to rip your stomach out with a machete."

I hung up.

In the end, I did get to keep Jessie for Wednesday night. Chad claimed he had just used a figure of speech, that it hadn't meant anything. But since he works on Wall Street, and not a martial arts academy, it seemed like a strange choice of words. In any case, words do mean something. These meant that no matter how much time elapsed between us things would never change, I would stand for only one thing for him. The phrase stayed in my mind, glittering and vicious, like a barracuda in a pool.

When I went downstairs to the kitchen, my father was banging around in there. Someone must have lit a fire in the library, and there was a comforting smell of wood smoke. Nick had gone running. My father turned and smiled at me when I came in, his brilliant blue eyes lighting up his face. He is nearly my height now, gentle, slow, and white-haired. This is always a shock to me: I still expect the towering giant of my childhood, stern and immutable.

"Hello, sweetie," he said.

"Hi, Daddy," I said, "sleep well?"

"Marvelously, thanks," he said. "So did your mother.

Her back has been bad lately, so she's going to stay in bed for a bit. I took her up some tea a while ago, and she's having a blissful time."

My mother, who is smaller than my small father, insists on the joy she finds in her days, and ignores the pain she feels in her back. I was glad to think of her resting, her thin, dark hair spread out in a hieroglyph of comfort and luxury against the wide white pillows in the guest room, my mother slowly sipping her tea with our house quiet around her. I offered the picture to Chad in my mind.

I looked into the library, but it was dark, and the deep chairs were empty. The wood smoke smell was stronger than ever.

In the kitchen my father held up a fragile English mochaware mug and a gold-rimmed dessert plate I had set out for dinner. "I guess you don't care what plates I use for breakfast," he said.

"Actually—" I said, and dived into the pantry for the everyday stuff. I handed him a thick pottery plate and mug, and put the mochaware back. I went over to the stove. The kettle was on fire.

"The kettle's on fire," I said, and snatched it up. Nick bought me that kettle in England, years ago. It has a wonderful shape, a long Art Deco curve of heavy metal, echoed by the long smooth arch of the solid wooden handle. It was the solid wooden handle that was giving off the comforting smell of wood smoke. I held the kettle under the running water at the sink. It made a terrible hissing sound.

"Kettle?" my father said. He was pulling out the canisters from where they stood against the blue-and-white checkerboard tiles: tea, instant coffee, lentils, navy beans.

"It's ruined," I said loudly, the gloom advancing. My father ambled over to the sink and peered at the kettle.

57

"I don't think it's ruined," he said reassuringly. I waited for him to make this true. "See," he said, "the bottom's still flat. We burnt one out, once, and the bottom turned inside out. This one's still flat."

But I shook my head. I knew ruin when I saw it. He was talking about a different kind of kettle, one of those flimsy whistle ones with the copper bottoms. "It's the handle," I said, "look at it." I wiggled the handle. It was very loose, and the wrong color. The air was full of the smell of charred wood.

My father shook his head, rubbing the back of his neck. "Well," he said, puzzled, "I wonder how it could have happened." I didn't say anything. "I turned it on myself when I made your mother tea, but that was a while ago. I know I turned it off again. Maybe Nick put it on afterward."

Despair began to enfold me in its dank embrace. I threw the kettle into the trash drawer and slammed it shut. There were tears behind my eyelids. Nick appeared from outside, his hands on his hips, breathing in deep slow breaths. His blond hair was damp from the drizzle, and there were shining drops on his eyebrows. He gave off heat and comfort like a god in sweat pants. He smiled.

"Morning, Sam," he said. "Hi, lovey. What's that smell?"

"The kettle's ruined," I said. "Someone left it on the stove and the handle's burned out." I had my back to him, not wanting to confront him with what he'd done.

"Oh, lovey," Nick said, unrepentant. "That's too bad."

I turned around. "Didn't you do it?"

"Turn on the kettle and then go out running? Of course not."

It was my father, then, and he wasn't even paying any attention. I turned back to the sink and wrenched the water on in a torrent. My beautiful kettle was destroyed, Jessie was gone, and Chad, or his wife, wanted to rip my stomach out with a machete.

My father was heating up water in a saucepan.

"I don't know how that could have happened," he said. "Someone must have turned it back on again after I went upstairs." I didn't say anything. "Unless I left it on myself," my father said, "but I can't imagine that I did." There was a pause. "But maybe I did."

I said nothing. Nick could see the blackness hovering around me. He came over and put his arms around me; it was like being grabbed by a strong damp quilt. He hugged me harder and harder until I hugged him back. "She'll be back on Sunday," he whispered. "It's only four days."

Maybe so, but in the meantime there was gloom all around me, and a houseful of people expecting me to present them with Thanksgiving.

"I don't know what's the matter with this coffee," my father said crossly, "I've put about five spoonfuls of it into my hot water, and it doesn't change color."

I peered over Nick's shoulder at the canister my father had gotten out.

"It's millet," I said, "you're pouring millet into your water."

"*Millet*," my father said, faintly outraged. He took his mug over to the sink and poured in the whole mess, where it would, I happened to know, stop things up.

Nick turned me loose and went to the sink as my father returned to the stove for a fresh try at the coffee. Nick started clearing up the soggy millet with his hands. He began to whistle. He was in a good mood because his children were on their way to us.

*   *   *

Chris and Jed are nineteen, good athletes and bad students. They are darker than Nick, and more solid, but they have the same large grin and important eyebrows. They come into our house and transform the space in it, these two large, peaceful bodies, leaning and sprawling and hustling against each other. Things don't trouble them: not grades, not divorce, not anything much. In some miraculous way they have forgiven both their parents for the divorce and let it all slide away, as though it were a failed algebra exam from last term. Jessie worships them.

Sophie is sixteen and has forgiven no one anything. At least she has forgiven Nick nothing. She has been to our house once in the last two years; the twins come by about once a month. Last spring she wrote Nick to ask if he would take her to Boston on the weekend of her birthday. Nick was thrilled. He wrote off for theater tickets, and got reservations at the Ritz. Then he didn't hear from her again. He couldn't reach her, and she didn't call. Finally, two days before the weekend she called to say she was going to New York for the weekend to stay with her mother. Sophie said she'd forgotten, when she wrote him, that she'd already made plans with her mother. She didn't even say she was sorry.

Nick had forgotten all this. What he was thinking about, whistling, scraping up the soggy millet, was how great Thanksgiving was going to be. How all of us would sit around the big polished elm wood table bright with expectation while he carved the goose. All he could see was how things would go right between himself and Sophie, how he would say nothing about her plummeting grades, nothing about her nutsy mother, nothing except how fond he was of her. And how she, Sophie, would suddenly have changed: she would be open, talking to all of us, laughing, and letting her father see how fond she was of him, telling stories about school, and showing us we were part of her life.

By the time Nick came back from the station with the children, the goose was in, and the warm, rich smell of it was beginning to drift through the house. I had driven off the black shroud, and was concentrating hard on things going well.

My father had taken over one end of the butcher-block counter. He had covered it with Duco cement tubes, screwdrivers, little jars of things, bits of other things, pieces of the kettle. He was repairing it.

When they came back from the station it was like a thunderstorm moving into the kitchen, jackets and duffel bags, all those big new bodies, careful gestures, the boys' deep voices, open smiles, and Sophie's tense, closed face.

We all kissed and shambled about, things were dropped on the floor. Chris leaned into a doorway and put his hands on the corners of the lintels. He swung there, grinning. Jed began to crack his knuckles, slowly. It sounded as though he were dislocating every joint.

"Ouch," I said, and winced, ritually.

"Sorry, Kate," he said, grinning at me. "Well," he said, and looked at Jed. "Guess it's about that time."

"What time?" I asked.

At the same time Nick asked, "Who's playing?"

"Dad," Jed said, "how can you ask that question? It's the All-Star Blitz!" One of the great blessings of my life is that Nick does not like to watch football.

The three of them went into the library to watch the kickoff—Nick would sit with them if they were watching hamster races. My father and Sophie and I were left alone in the kitchen.

Sophie is shorter than I, solid and dark like her brothers, but less agile, less graceful. She seems attached to the ground, wary, as though any kind of departure is a risk she cannot take. She had bare legs, and was wearing a wrinkled denim skirt and a rumpled jersey that slid off her shoulder and showed her bra straps. Usually, when she comes to our house she goes straight to her room, closes the door, and puts on her Walkman. She stays there in isolation until someone goes up and bangs on the door and insists that she come down. But this time I had planned something for her, something mild and low-key that might ease her into Thanksgiving with us.

"Want to help me make the pecan pie?" I asked. "I'll do the pie crust, and you do the filling?"

"Okay," Sophie said neutrally. I showed her the recipe. Everything was out, waiting for her, the bag of pecans, bowls, the nutcracker. She started cracking nuts, and I started on the pastry.

Making pastry is not what I'm good at. I make all our bread, so you might think I could do pastry but I can't. They're very different things. Bread dough loves to be kneaded, you can pound and pound and pound it and it comes out right. But pastry can't bear to be handled, and too much fussing will ruin it altogether. What I'm not good at is leaving things alone, knowing when to stop.

I mixed the dry ingredients together, flour and salt, and began to measure the lard. "So," I said cheerfully, "how's school?"

"Good," Sophie said. She didn't look up. I had seen the report card: straight D's.

"That's good," I said. "I hope you're feeling better than you were when you wrote that letter." She had written us a sad little note about feeling lonely.

"Oh, yeah," Sophie said, shrugging her shoulders. "I was just down when I wrote that. I don't even know why I wrote it."

"Well, good," I said, rebuffed.

Nick came back from the library. He stood next to Sophie and put his arm around her.

"You're pretty good at that, aren't you," he said. Sophie was taking out the pecans whole, intact, from the shells.

"Thanks," she said, without looking up.

"Look at that," he said, "what hands." He started to kiss her along her temple, just along the hairline, little tiny kisses. I chopped away with the pastry blender, hoping. What I wanted was the right texture. I wanted everything smooth, the silky flour accepting the soft, frail slips of lard.

"Well, Sophe," Nick said, "we've been talking about taking a trip next summer, the whole family. We'd go all around Spain. What do you think?"

Nick loves planning trips. I looked up. Sophie still had her head down. She was eating one of the broken pecans.

"Fine," she said. Her voice was noncommittal. It was clear that the trip to Spain—that the phrase *the whole family*—did not include her, did not have anything to do with her at all. She would not be blended into anything.

"Wouldn't that be fun, don't you think?" Nick went on. He was still smiling at her, he still had his arm around her. I started pouring the ice water, little by little, into the flour and water. This was the tricky part. If you put in too much water you end up with a horrible gluey mass that sticks to everything. If you don't add enough, the whole thing falls apart when you try to roll it out, a pile of disinterested, unconnected crumbs.

"So what do you think, Sophe?" Nick said again, and Sophie shrugged her shoulders.

"I don't know," she said, concentrating on her pecans. "I've never been to Spain."

Nick took his arm away from her. "I didn't ask you if you'd ever been to Spain," he said. "I asked you if you thought it would be fun, all of us taking a trip together." Sophie tossed a handful of shells into the bowl. Some of them missed, and went onto the floor. She ignored them. I dabbed gingerly at the pastry with my fingertips. "Would Jessie be coming?" Sophie asked.

"Of course Jessie would be coming," Nick said. He loves Jessie. "We would all be going. What I'm asking you is whether or not you think that would be fun."

"I don't *know*, Dad," she said, determined. "*Maybe*."

I sloshed a little more ice water into the mixture, and sunk my fingertips in.

"Well, we don't have to decide this minute," I said. Sophie glanced at me. I smiled at her but she looked down again. I dabbed some more at the pastry. I was trying not to ruin it. "I'm sure it will be fun," I said in a general way.

Nick stepped away from Sophie and crossed his arms on his chest. His mouth had gone into a straight line.

My father appeared at my elbow. He held the kettle up to me proudly. "There," he said, "I've fixed it." The kettle hung uneasily from the wooden handle; the joint was loose and wiggly.

"Thank you, Daddy," I said.

"I scraped out all the charred part," my father explained, "and I glued in a wooden match stick, and then you see I screwed that into the joint. That's how I could make it tight enough for the screw to hold."

"That's wonderful," I said, "thank you very much." I dabbed at the pastry.

"Sophie," I said, chatty, "give us the scoop on Allie. How is she?"

Allie is Sophie's one friend from school who lives near us. As soon as she and Sophie became friends, however, her parents split up and Allie's mother moved to New York, so Sophie sees her there instead of in the country from our house.

"She's good," Sophie said, nodding. "Oh, I meant to tell you," she said, turning to Nick. "I told Allie I'd spend the night with her tonight. So could you drive me there after dinner?"

Nick said nothing. They faced each other. Nick's eyebrows were pulled in toward each other, his mouth was at an ominous angle. Sophie's eyes were hooded and uninvolved, and her eyebrows rose to a central peak of disinterest.

"When are you going back to New York?" Nick asked.

Sophie shrugged. "I guess tomorrow morning," she said. "I have a lot of things to do."

Nick stared at her. "So," he said, "you'll be here for what, about six hours? Is that it?"

Sophie didn't answer.

"You come out here for the first time in two years, you're here for one night, and you have to spend that night with a girl you see every day at school?"

Sophie went on with the pecans. I had to admit she was dexterous: not one of them was broken.

My father was still holding the kettle. "In fact," he said quietly, mostly to himself, "now that I know how to do it, I think I'll make it a bit tighter."

He took the kettle away again. I patted gingerly at the dough. It was all mixed. I took it out of the bowl and set it down on the floured marble slab as though it were made of nitroglycerine.

65

"Why don't you set the table for lunch," I said to Nick. I wanted to get him away from Sophie.

"Right," he said, still looking at Sophie. "How many are we? Are you going to be here for lunch, Sophie, or is there some friend's house you'd rather dash off to? Two meals in a row in your father's house is a lot to ask, I know."

I began to roll the dough out with the old-fashioned rolling pin, its rich, dark wood taking a firm commanding weight against the difficult dough.

"Well, I hope you are staying for lunch, Sophe," I said briskly, "we're counting on you." My voice sounded strained and terrible in my own ears, but she looked up briefly and smiled at me.

"Yeah," she said, "I'll be here."

It wasn't going to be great, I could see that. It wasn't falling apart, but it was a bit sticky, and I slid the spatula underneath it between each roll, to make sure it wasn't gluing itself to the marble. You can't just add more flour when it's sticky. You can ruin it that way, too. I sprinkled a bit of flour on the rolling pin, and kept on pushing it out into bigger and bigger circles. Finally I got the pie plate out to measure it, but the circle wasn't big enough yet. And it wasn't evenly round, either. I'd have to patch parts of it, and the rim would be ragged. But I can only make what I can make.

"Put out places for everyone," I said firmly to Nick, and to Sophie I said, "It should be fun for you to see Allie at her dad's. You've never seen her out here, have you?"

My father appeared at my side again. He was holding up the kettle and smiling, but his eyes looked as though someone had hit him, they were bruised and painful.

"Sorry," he said gently, "I've ruined it."

I looked at the kettle. He had, he'd ruined it again. The handle was now attached at only one end. He had bored out so much of the charred wood that the hole was too big to fill. No screw would hold it.

"Oh, Daddy," I said.

"I'd like to buy you a new one," he said.

"Don't be silly," I said, sliding the spatula beneath the dough. It stuck, then yielded. I pressed down on the rolling pin for these last determined surges.

"No, really, I would," my father said. "It would make me feel better about it. I don't want you to think of me as someone who comes to your house and breaks things, and walks away."

Then I turned and looked at my father, whose eyes are now nearly on a level with mine. He stood there waiting for my answer, one eyebrow raised hopefully. He has become so gentle that I can hardly bear it, and he needed something from me. I put my arms around him, my hands meeting unexpectedly soon behind his back. Second chances, that's all we can hope for, and when we find them, grab.

NIGHT VISION

ℜ

The *couchette* from Paris to Interlaken leaves from the Gare
de Lyon just before midnight. The station at that hour is
vast and gloomy, and, to Steven, their group seemed noisy
and brash, invading the deep spaces with careless noise.
Everyone seemed to have come on with them from the restaurant, though only Steven, his wife, Lisa, and Clive were
getting on the train.

Walking down the long platform, Steven listened to the
steady hollow echo of their footsteps. Clive was in front, like
a general leading his troops. He was an old friend of Lisa's,
an English journalist who lived in Paris. He wore blue jeans,
cowboy boots, and a camel's-hair coat thrown over his shoulders like a cape. Lisa walked beside him, her long legs in
high purple boots, a fringed shawl thrown over her jacket.
They were arguing, as usual.

"You are so arrogant," Lisa said, "you Brits are all so
arrogant." Steven could not hear Clive's answer. Lisa took a
rapid, skipping step to keep up, and the fringe on her shawl
swung angrily.

Next to Steven walked a sulky French girl with short,

gleaming hair, and on the other side of her was the Italian who wanted to buy a vineyard in California. They were all Clive's friends, they, and the English couple who wrote screenplays, and the rich Portuguese Clive played tennis with. Steven and Lisa had met them for the first time at the crowded, smoky restaurant near the Madeleine.

Steven had sat between the English couple, who had ignored him completely, quarreling steadily across him. At least this had relieved him of making an effort at conversation; he was deeply tired. He had spent the last two days at the Paris office of his company's law firm: an annual task, annually exhausting. The sudden flood of French and the long row of decisions to be made had worn him out. Walking down the platform he felt suspended in exhaustion like a diver in deep water, all sound and connections gone. He longed to be on the train, rolled in a blanket, rocked in darkness.

Steven blinked his eyes. They felt, not exactly painful, but there was an ache, some sense of dull unease he could not quite name. He squinted in the dim light: some trick of the shadows, or the echoing spaces, or perhaps it was the lateness of the hour that made it impossible to see certain things. He could not seem to focus on things at a certain distance, things he was—wasn't he?—accustomed to seeing clearly.

There was an invasive chill in the damp air, and Steven hunched his shoulders against it. The voices of Clive and Lisa rose and faded, sliding in and out of his consciousness like a radio left on in another room. He heard Clive say politely, "Oh, you have universities in America, do you?" and then he heard him laugh; he wondered what Lisa had done.

The three of them were going skiing in Switzerland,

though Steven, rumpled, cold, tired, in the endless gloom of the midnight station, could not now imagine why. The Paris trip usually took place in the summer, but this year it had been changed to March. When Steven had heard this, he had wondered if he should go over alone, and plan another trip with Lisa in the summer.

They had discussed it one night in their kitchen, Steven in his shirtsleeves and his old corduroys, leaning against the white painted table, waiting for dinner. The table was already set; Lisa had given him a white nineteen-twenties plate, with stylized baskets of yellow flowers around the rim. She had given herself an old, crackled blue-and-white rose pattern: her china was all bought singly at junk shops, and none of her plates matched. Lisa stood at the big old-fashioned stove on its high legs. On either side of it the wooden cabinets, glass-fronted, reached up to the ceiling. Lisa's assortment of china was dimly visible through the panes.

"Paris in March won't be any fun," said Steven. "Maybe I should just go over and come back, and you and I can go together later, in the summer."

Lisa shook her head impatiently, pushing her hair away from her face with her forearm. Steven stepped forward and put his arms around her from behind. He put his face into her hair, the cloudy mass of it, faintly rough, like soft grass. She leaned against him, and he moved his hands across the strong arch of her ribs. Over her shoulder Steven could see the trembling blue circles of flame beneath the pots, he could feel the heat coming up at his face. He felt the small shifts and tensions in Lisa's thighs, in her shoulders, as she leaned forward to stir something. She was making a risotto, and the smell of the cheese, the stock, rose up at him with the steamy heat. Lisa's shoulders were against his chest, and he felt the soft rise of her rump against his thighs. He liked holding his wife from behind: it allied him with her, it put them on the same side.

"Oh, no," said Lisa, "don't go alone. Let's not waste the trip."

"But it will be cold and damp, everywhere, even if we go to the south of France, or Italy."

"Well, we can go somewhere it's meant to be cold. We'll go skiing."

"Skiing," said Steven.

"Why not?"

"I haven't skied in years," said Steven. "I don't ski."

"You do," said Lisa, "you just don't."

It was true that Steven had skied years ago, before his first marriage. He had given it up when he married; his first wife had disliked it, and they had gone south for winter vacations. Now the whole process of skiing seemed cold and cumbersome, part of someone else's life. He was trying to put his past behind him, he was addressing this new life, Lisa. They had been married for two years, and were still finding things out about each other.

Lisa was a graphic designer, she was from California, and she was ten years younger than Steven. She was smart and energetic and funny. She seemed interested in everything. She took easily things that he thought were serious, seriously things he thought were insignificant. She loved opera, which he found daunting, and she thought duck shooting silly, which he found faintly wounding. She liked baseball, and could recite the history, all the statistics, of each of the players. She had served on the Santa Monica School Board, she had taught art classes in London, she had bred Australian sheep dogs. She had no children, and would not discuss it (something had gone wrong, years ago). She took for granted both the importance of her job and of his happiness: this was the most remarkable thing about Lisa, for Steven. She loved him. He was amazed at this, and grateful. Not only did she love him, she loved him strenuously: she confronted him with herself, she made inescapable the fact that she loved him. At night she slept clambered boldly about his body, each move he made was encumbered, involved, with her soft light limbs. She wrapped herself into his life, his nights, she made him quicken.

Three years earlier Steven had left his first wife and his daughter in their old apartment on East Seventy-second Street. When he took up with Lisa he moved across town, into her apartment on West End Avenue. Steven had never lived on the West Side, and this felt like a bold political move. Lisa's building had high ceilings and graceful moldings, like Steven's old apartment, but, instead of a grand piano in the living room, there was Lisa's drafting table, austere, angular, functional. On the wall, instead of English horticultural prints, she had hung something she had found in a junkyard: the old Pontiac symbol, a huge metal Indian head in silhouette. It was still rusty around the edges, and Steven had suggested that they send it to a restorer, but Lisa said it was the roughness that she liked.

The Indian head, like the neighborhood, seemed to have undergone some mysterious gentrification process. It was not the kind of thing he had grown up with, and Steven was never sure what to make of it. Sometimes it seemed a tawdry relic—junk, really—the symbol of a steamy, seamy decade, one of scarlet lips and adolescent passions. Sometimes it seemed serious, a classical silhouette, an ideal of speed and nobility. But he liked this, its mutability, and the idea of seeing things in a new way excited him. He was grateful to Lisa, for changing his life, for bringing him these new visions. And she, like the Indian, was full of mysterious shifts, unexpected views. Why did she buy used plates from sidewalk sales and junk shops, instead of from a proper china store? And what about the rusty edges on the Indian head? He was used to having things clean, things arranged so that you were in charge of them, so you knew what they were. These shifts that Lisa brought to him were exhilarating but unsettling.

"I'm not from your tribe, that's all." Lisa told him. She had majored in anthropology at Berkeley. "These are tribal differences between us, not ethical ones." Sometimes Steven did feel as though he were with a member of some wild tribe, she seemed so full of conviction, so knowledgeable about such strange things. He felt bewildered and tentative, he had no choice but to trust her.

Standing in the kitchen, Steven felt reluctant at her suggestion. "Skiing," he said. He had given it up, years ago. He felt too old to start all that up again, the risks of those steep, cold slopes.

"Clive will know somewhere to go," Lisa said decisively, "I'll call him tomorrow."

"You don't have to call Clive to find a place for us to go skiing," Steven said, nettled. "I can find a place for us to go."

Lisa looked at him at once and smiled. "All right," she said. "I know that."

And there they left it, Steven thought, but the next day Clive called Steven at his office. Clive had just been talking to Lisa, he said, and she had mentioned their plan to go skiing. He thought he should tell Steven about a little village in the Bernese Oberlands, beneath the famous Eiger, where there were old-fashioned pensions, broad treeless *pistes*, wonderful food, and no cars.

"It sounds very nice," said Steven politely.

"It is rather sweet, actually," Clive said. "You get there

on the night train from Paris, and change at Interlaken. And there's one little inn in particular that I know, I think you'd like it."

"I wonder if it would be hard to book all that this late in the season."

"I've already called the pension," said Clive, "and I've found out about the train. Everything is still available. I'll book it for us from here if you like."

"Ah, you're coming with us, are you?" Steven asked, irritated.

"If you can bear it. Lisa very kindly suggested that you might be able to. But tell me if you'd rather be alone. I'd love to see you both, and as it happens I'll be between things then. But do please say if you'd rather be *à deux*."

"It's only that I wasn't altogether sure that we had decided to go," said Steven.

"Ah," said Clive, "I had the impression that you were— rather decided."

"Not actually, no," said Steven bluntly, trying to kill some of Clive's grace. "The thing is, I'm not much of a skier."

"Nor am I, I assure you," Clive said instantly. "You and I shall link arms and make cautious snowplow turns down the slope, waving sedately to Lisa as she schusses past us with her dashing Swiss guide, full of schnapps."

Steven laughed. He liked Clive, it would be churlish to rebuff him. And he knew what would happen with Lisa: she would be incredulous at his irritation. She had tried to reach him, he was in a meeting, then she was in a meeting, Clive was only being friendly, and, in any case, didn't it sound very nice? Steven had to admit that it did sound nice. But when he hung up he had a moment of real dread—could it be wise, this return to those icy runs, risk-filled descents? He thought of the serious cold of the deep snow, of the dooming overhangs of rocks. He suddenly remembered pictures he had seen of the fearful Eiger, looming like a vast skull over the village below.

The group shifted during its passage down the platform, and Steven found himself again, impossibly, walking between the English husband and wife, who continued their feud.

"I think you might have *told* me," the woman said bitterly, before Steven realized she was there. He turned, startled, to her, and met the look she was sending to her husband. Steven took it full in his face, like acid.

He quickened his steps to get away from them, and hunched his shoulders against the cold. Even so, the damp reached in at him, and he shivered. They would never reach the train, it seemed, the night would pass in this interminable march. Steven peered ahead: trying to penetrate the gloomy tunnel, he was again aware that his eyes were working oddly. He squinted, past Clive's authoritative back, past the camel's-hair coat, swaying briskly.

"I like New York," he heard Clive say magnanimously. "I find the people there interesting. Not more intelligent than the people here—they're not—but *interesting.*"

"Gosh, how kind," said Lisa. "They'll be so pleased to hear that."

There was some itch between Clive and Lisa. Whatever they discussed, they disagreed on. They carried on like siblings, not angrily, but as though they could not help themselves, a steady undercurrent of heated irritation between them. Steven had once asked Lisa if she had gone out with Clive. She had laughed.

"I was married then," she said. "I was married to Robert. I wasn't going out with people." She had not said no.

Steven did not pursue it. Lisa's past, like Steven's, was

75

now too large to own. Their first marriages loomed, dangerous passages, in their adult lives. He had owned his first wife's past, he knew her early loves, her childhood, and he had offered up his own. But he and Lisa each had a great failure behind them—there were things he could not bear to know about her, and things of his own he would rather not share, there was censure he would rather not endure from her as well as from himself. There was the problem of his daughter, who would barely speak to him: he would not discuss the mistakes he had made.

Second marriages had this lack of transparency: there were things better not brought to light. The brave certainty of the first marriage, the conviction that love would overcome any revelation—Steven still held that notion, but he held it in private. He preferred not to test it. He held Lisa in the center of his life, he did not need to know all the pain in her past. At forty-eight, he hoped those things were over, hoped they were past confrontations, past violent revelations. He wanted now to live peacefully with his wife.

"Here we are," Clive called out briskly, "a mere four and a half miles from the station. Walk after dinner, good for the digestion." They were, at last, in front of the train, they were even in front of the right car. Everyone stood about on the platform. Metallic steam drifted up in clouds from the wheels of the train; the pavement gleamed with damp. The light was greenish, deep shadows cut across faces. Color had been sucked from the scene, and everyone was gaunt and hollow-eyed, like vampires. Steven had the sense of nightmare.

Animated by the prospect of an ending, people began to talk in different languages. The Italian began to sing a French song, and the Portuguese joined in, putting his arm across the Italian's shoulder. Their voices were enormous in the

shadowy space. The light came down from directly overhead, and behind was blackness, so they seemed onstage.
The song was about "le départ," but they did not know most
of the words, and much of the time they sang "la-la-la,"
instead, roaring with laughter. It was endless, Steven
thought, he was trapped in this forever. He longed simply
to climb onto the train, but Clive stood on the top step of
the car, smiling. Lisa stood on the step below. The two of
them looked like celebrities, movie stars on tour. Lisa wore
a soft felt hat that shadowed her eyes, and the fringed shawl
muffled her neck and framed her face. In the shadows her
eyes shone, and Steven could see the whiteness of her smile.
She raised her hand to throw a kiss to the singers, and lost
her balance slightly on the narrow step. Clive put his arm
around her, finding the curve of her body so easily that
Steven, watching, felt an odd catch in his breathing.

Clive leaned over, laughing, talking to the singers. He
was handsome, in an English way: tall, very blond, with a
narrow, bony face. Steven was suddenly filled with a dislike
for his looks, those weedy, overbred features, the supercilious
expression, the overcoat thrown over the shoulders.

"Could we get on, do you think, any time soon?" Steven
asked.

Clive turned to him at once, taking his hands off Lisa's
shoulders without haste, clear-eyed, polite.

"This instant," Clive said, half-bowing. He called good-
bye in a last general way, and turned in toward the train.
Lisa smiled at Steven, too, putting her hand on his shoulder
as he came up the steps to her. Steven mounted without
saying good-bye to the others, he had had enough of them,
and he was tired. Also, he had not liked the sight of Lisa
and Clive waving glamorously.

Inside the train, at once, all was different. The space was

intimate, tiny, enclosed. They could hear one another breathing. A conductor appeared in an ornate uniform, buckled, trimmed, buttoned, his mustache a neat line. His face was impeccably composed, he was full of conviction.

"*Vos passeports, Madame, Messieurs,*" the conductor said crisply. Silently they handed them over. The conductor opened them, nodded, and tucked them inside his jacket. He strode off down the narrow corridor.

"Will we ever see them again, do you think?" Lisa said. "Why won't he just sell them on the black market in East Berlin?"

"We're going nowhere near East Berlin, Lisa," Steven said, irritably, nudging her toward their cabin. He was longing for sleep.

The compartment had four bunks: two up, two down. A Swiss with a fierce mustache lay in a lower one, the blanket pulled neatly to his chest, his eyes shut. Steven sat down on the other lower bunk and began to unlace his shoes.

"This is wonderful," Lisa whispered loudly. She pulled off her boots and clambered easily into the bunk above Steven. Clive climbed up more sedately into the bunk across from her. Steven, watching, wondered how old Clive was. Somewhere between himself and Lisa, probably, early forties. Up on his bunk, Clive pulled off his tooled cowboy boots and dropped them on the floor. Steven put his smooth black business shoes side by side beneath his bunk. Cowboy boots, he thought.

Overhead, Lisa ranged about in her bunk, settling herself in like a dog in deep grass.

"Isn't this great?" she asked, her head appearing suddenly above Steven's, smiling. The overhead light shone directly above her, he could barely see her face.

"It's great," said Steven, smiling. He took off his jacket, and slid his suspenders off his shoulders. He unpacked the couchette kit: a clean, coarse cotton pillowcase, a thick red wool blanket. He took off his trousers and stuffed his clothes at the foot of the bunk. He lay down, still in his shirt, and pulled the blanket up. He could not quite stretch his legs out completely, and felt cramped and restless.

Lisa was whispering to Clive. "It's like the Orient Express, isn't it. Here we are at midnight, with no passports, and a spy in the bottom bunk."

Of course she meant the Swiss. Steven hoped he didn't speak English.

"Is there a murder every night, do you think? What a nuisance for the gendarmes!"

Steven lay on his back, staring at the bunk-bottom above him. There was a small mirror on it, pointlessly reflecting his blanket. He felt something touch his face: Lisa's fingers. He looked up to see her face hanging raggedly upside down: she was smiling at him. The light glared through her hair, a dusky red cloud.

Steven smiled back. "There's a mirror on my ceiling."

"There's not!" said Lisa. "What are they thinking of? Aren't murders enough for them?"

Steven laughed. "I think it's meant for daytime, when the bunk is up against the wall and the mirror is vertical."

"Still, it seems a shame to waste it now," Lisa said. "Shall I come down?"

"Do," Steven invited.

Her fingertips moved across his face, and he felt her reminding herself of his flesh, the shape of his face, the pleasure she took in it: the rise of his cheeks, the hollow of his temple. She stroked the hair back gently from his temples, touched his lips. Steven kissed her fingers, hard, he held them to his mouth and pressed them, warm, against his cheek.

"I love you," whispered Lisa.

"I love you," he whispered back. "Good night."

"Good night." She smiled down at him.

Steven raised his voice. "Good night, Clive." Clive's face appeared, long and sheepy, over the edge of his bunk.

"Good night, Steven. I imagine we'll all sleep blissfully until Interlaken, where we will pull up the shades to discover our luggage neatly stacked with the utmost Swiss efficiency onto the wrong platform as we steam irrevocably away from it."

"Something to look forward to," Steven said, smiling at him, too.

"Will the light bother you?" Lisa asked them both. "There's only this big overhead one, and I have to read for a bit or I won't be able to sleep."

"Oh, God, you're one of those," Clive said easily.

"It won't bother me," Steven said. He didn't like Clive classifying Lisa among women with whom he had spent the night, he didn't like Clive knowing Lisa's bedtime habits.

Rolling back up on top of her bunk, Lisa was now invisible to her husband. She said something Steven could not hear, and Clive laughed. Then there was silence, and Steven wondered what they were doing, the two of them, on those high, private, lighted bunks. He wondered if they were smiling at each other, if Clive were looking at Lisa's face on the pillow, her hair spread out across that white linen.

Steven rolled toward the wall, pulling the blanket up to his chin and closing his eyes, willing himself to sleep. The train had begun to move, silently at first, slipping like water underneath the streets of Paris at night, then picking up a more determined, businesslike rhythm, clicking and sway-ing. Dozing, waiting for sleep, Steven opened his eyes, stared dimly at the wall, closed them again. The sliding rattle of the train made it difficult to hear anything else, but he found himself listening for conversation overhead. There were times when he was sure he heard laughter. He became con-vinced that part of the humming rattle around him was the steady undercurrent of conversation. They were talking, he was sure of it: on and on. He opened his eyes. The light was still on. He imagined them laughing, lying on their pillows, watching each other. Why did they not just go to sleep? What were they thinking of? He imagined complaining to them, standing up and speaking sternly to them, like a teacher.

Of course he wouldn't: he would sound like Lisa's father. It was possible they were not talking at all. Possibly he was hearing mechanical gibberish, not conversation. He would lie quietly in his bunk, not stand up and see what was go-ing on.

Steven opened his eyes, he was not as sleepy as he had thought. Looking around his cramped space he thought again of the odd sensation he had had on the platform. He would experiment again here. He focused first, firmly, on his hand, holding the blanket. He saw it clearly: the skin was pale, bluish in the dim light, the knuckles taut, blunt, the deep fleshy creases of the curled-up fingers definite. He opened his hand: the fingers seemed thicker, somehow, than he ex-pected. He flexed them, and something—the way they moved, or the set of the bones inside the flesh—reminded him of his father's hands as he had lain dying in the hospital, those thickened, twisted shapes. At the hospital he had looked at the hands, forgiving his father for the frailty of his flesh, but he could see now that his own hands possessed, in fearful embryo, that same shape, potential for the same thickened worthlessness. Steven flattened his hand out on the blanket, strong and rigid. He made the hand his own, willing the image shift, like the Indian head, to one he wanted: the hands he remembered from his youth, large, supple, strong.

Steven looked farther down the bunk, to the hump of one knee beneath the blanket. He could see distinctly the weave of the wool, the diagonal strokes in it. He felt cheered, as though he could, simply by willpower, clear up this physical problem.

He shifted his gaze confidently to the post at the foot of his bunk, and found confusion. The outline of the post—a simple black shaft—was vague and blurry. Even worse, there seemed to be two outlines, each edge seemed vaguely doubled. Squinting, concentrating, Steven tried to reconcile the lines, to draw them magically into each other with his will: he could not. He tried again, first with one eye, then the other. It was so strange an effort, involving muscles he did not know how to command, energy he did not know how to direct. He found himself holding his breath, straining, frowning. The lines were unresolved.

The discovery was so large, so flat and disturbing that at first Steven simply rejected it. It was like the problem, always with him, of leaving Amanda, his daughter. The knowledge that he could never correct that error, never make up for it, had damaged Steven. He could see now that he could not reconcile these shifting lines, he could not make them take on the appearance of true reality which he knew was there. He was helpless, now, and it frightened him. Amanda would continue, surly, hostile, aligned with his first wife against him. His eyesight would get worse. What was he going toward?

The overhead light went out above him, but the cabin was not black. From his bunk Steven could see the safety light, a small red bulb that sent out a dull, surreal glow, dim but insistent.

Lisa and Clive must be going to sleep. Steven listened, but could tell no change in the undercurrent of mutterings. Perhaps he had been mistaken, after all, perhaps they had not talked at all. He longed for Lisa to reach down again to touch his face, he longed to tell her of the danger he had discovered.

The sense of loss, the unexpected treason of his own body, shook him. There was nothing he could do, his body was aging. All of him was aging, without his consent, all of him was changing, whether he noticed it or not, whether he permitted it or not. Of course, he had always known this, he was not such a fool as to think he would not grow older, but—what? He had not thought it would happen so soon, or with such brutality, that there would be no appeal. And there was Lisa: Steven could see that on some private, illogical level he had believed that by allying himself with Lisa's freshness, her quicksilver energy, that he had somehow acquired some of it himself—youth by association.

Now the fallacy of this was borne in on him, chilling. He was becoming older; Lisa had no part in it; he was alone.

Steven lay very still in the dim red glare. Above him the subtle current of noise continued: were they talking? He kept himself immobile, separate, as though by forbidding himself motion he could somehow alter the inclination of tissue, of bone and cartilage and blood vessel. He set himself against the thought of aging, as though he had a choice.

He began drifting toward sleep; he turned onto his side. As his mind began shifting in and out of consciousness, Steven found himself reaching out for Lisa. He missed the tanglement of her limbs. His drowsy hand groped for the loose, complicated connection of her body, trying to gather it to himself, trying to press the smooth descent of her spine to his chest. Each time, his hand touched the metal wall of the compartment, and he half-waked himself again. He was on a train, he was being carried through the depths of the night across the continent of Europe, through the countries of strangers, into a dour mountainous place whose language he could not speak.

The train stopped so subtly, gliding to such a gentle, tenuous pause, that Steven, waking, was not sure of anything: how long it had been stopped, how long he had been asleep, whether or not he was still asleep, in fact. The breathing silence of the train was absolute. There was the feeling of the utmost reaches of the night itself, that part of it which cannot be struggled against. But the silence, the cessation of the gliding passage of the train, kept Steven alert, as though he must keep some sort of vigil until the passage was resumed. And, as he lay still, the sullen glow of the red bulb permeating his tiny darkness, he became aware that the silence in his own cabin was alive. He became aware that in the bunk overhead Lisa was crying.

Lisa crying was very difficult to detect: she was silent, her breath slowly leaving her chest in a series of painful exhalations until she seemed empty altogether, only misery left inside her body. When she drew the next breath there was a sound, high, faint, private. It was that sound which Steven thought he heard now; he listened, waiting for it to come again, and it did.

Steven moved gently to the outer edge of his bunk and looked up. The red glow came from the center of the wall between the two bunks. The light changed everything, casting a scarlet dusk over everything it touched. Up above him, between the two bunks, Steven saw a shape, profoundly black, linking the beds. It was a silhouette: an arm. He stayed still. The train around him rocked faintly, faintly, poised in this nighttime stillness. He heard Clive's voice, so soft, so gentle, that it might be coming from next to Steven's own pillow, the night around them had become so intimate.

"But you were so brave when it happened," Clive said, "you didn't cry then."

Steven felt Lisa's descending breath, then heard the faint sad sound as she drew it in again.

"I wasn't brave," she said, "I was twenty-two years old. I didn't believe the doctor. I was sure I'd have children. I was sure I knew better than him."

Now Steven lay absolutely without moving, almost without drawing breath, as though a sound from him would mean the apocalypse. It was all he could do, really: be quiet.

CHARITY DANCE

The first thing that Laura saw as she came in the door that evening was the person too terrible to name, even to herself. Laura's gaze did not falter or even pause, sweeping smoothly right past the woman's face, past the man standing next to her, who had been Laura's husband for eight years and who was now the husband of the other woman. Laura's gaze was clear and her eye was mild, but the sight of those two people was like the sudden electrifying blast of a whistle, shattering the center of her. Everything that had been loose in Laura's body became taut. The proportions of the evening changed. Laura wondered if she could not simply turn around and slip right back out the door and onto the nighttime street.

But there were people crowding in behind her, she was jostled forward. Audrey Cunningham, who was on the committee, caught her eye and waved. It was too late, and Laura began unbuttoning her coat as she labored her way through the crush toward Audrey.

The two women kissed each other.

"Quite a crowd," said Laura.

"Isn't it awful?" asked Audrey, looking around. People were cramped into the narrow spaces between tables, looking uncomfortable already. "They lied to us about the number of people this place could take. Where is the Asiatic flu now that we need it?"

"But everything looks very nice," said Laura. "It's a pretty room."

"Bless you," said Audrey. "It is a pretty room, isn't it? And don't you love the palm trees? They cost the earth, and that wretched man refused to donate a cent to us—he wouldn't even give us wholesale prices."

Laura smiled but said nothing. The two women looked out again across the mass of people.

"Did you know James was coming?" asked Laura, not looking at Audrey.

Audrey turned to her. "Yes, of course I knew," she said. Laura said nothing. "Now, come on," said Audrey. "It's been *five years*. There will be two hundred people here tonight. You can handle that."

Laura shook her head and smiled. She still did not look at Audrey.

Audrey patted her shoulder. "You look terrific," she said. "I love your bag." She picked this up, as it hung from Laura's shoulder. "Is *it* divine. Where did you get it?"

The bag had the shape and texture of fine braided straw. It was like the little bags Laura had taken to church at Easter as a child, but this one was made of pure silver. It was quite beautiful; James had given it to her when they were first married.

"I've had it for years," said Laura.

"I love it," said Audrey. Her attention was going. "There's that idiot headwaiter. He's going to tell me we have too many people." Audrey went off into the crowd, her smooth brown back making a wide V into the waist of her red silk dress.

Left alone, Laura straightened her spine and lifted her chin. Her own dress had a sequined top, and made her (she hoped) look slim and dashing. Her hair was shiny, a glossy black cap that neatly framed her face. She looked around: she knew almost everyone she saw. These people were part of her life, she had met them at party after party, at drinks in friends' weekend houses, at tennis tournaments, at charity balls, at holiday cocktail parties. Laura smiled at people, nodding, as she moved through the crowd, pushing toward a group she wanted to stand with, a group who would welcome her, where a man would ask if he could get her a drink.

More and more people arrived: the noise was terrible. Laura, talking with her friends, smiled and laughed, throwing her head back and showing off her neck and shoulders. She never looked at them, but she was aware at every second where James and the other person were. She could see their silhouettes without looking, as though the images had been etched into her mind with acid. The woman's body, flat and angular, her fine mist of hair, her pale northern eyes burnt into Laura's consciousness like sparks into flesh. She was alien to Laura, utterly foreign: who was this awful creature that had maimed her life? What could she be like, what poison in her veins? For it had not been James's fault. No gesture of his had ruined the world that he and Laura had made. No matter what he had said, Laura knew it had been this intruder, this gleaming, wild, dangerous person, who had torn the smooth surface of their marriage. Laura could not risk looking at her.

At dinner Laura sat next to Michael Bannister, an old friend, whose wife Sarah had been at school with Laura.

"Where's Sarah?" asked Laura, "I didn't see her."

"She's in Santa Barbara with her mother," said Michael, but Laura leaned forward and shook her head, not hearing him. "I SAID SHE'S IN SANTA BARBARA WITH HER MOTHER!" said Michael. "This is really something!"

"Isn't it awful?" said Laura. "Audrey said they lied to her about the space."

Michael leaned very close to Laura and whispered in her ear, "If Audrey made the arrangements I'm surprised they were even expecting us tonight." Laura laughed, and moved slightly away from him. Michael was tall, with a Roman nose and thick black hair. He was very good-looking, he was very clever, and he was not quite kind. Since she had been divorced, Laura had seen some of her friends, men, in a new light. Men she had known for years, her friends, married to her friends, might, on a slow, hot night in the summer, or at the end of a long dinner party, when their wives were away, these men might ask themselves up to Laura's apartment for a drink. They might talk and drink and stay until there was no point in going home at all. This pained Laura. Seldom did she let them come up, and still less often did she let them stay, the married men. But sometimes, the velvet depths of the night enclosing her and concealing her idea of how things really ought to be, sometimes Laura simply gave in to the strain of having been abandoned, sometimes she turned to those arms, those married men, for comfort.

Laura had found that when she next saw the men they seemed faintly embarrassed but full of virtue, as though they had made a large donation to a charity but did not like to brag about it. Laura sensed this possibility in Michael.

"By the way," she said, "I want to thank you again for writing that school recommendation for Jamie. I'm so glad he's at Choate."

"Oh, you're quite welcome," said Michael, waving his hand. "I'm delighted he's gone there. When did he start?"

"Last week."

"And how's it going?"

Laura smiled and nodded, "I think well. It's a bit soon to tell." What was not going well was her suddenly empty apartment, her suddenly solitary life. She and Jamie had looked after each other, and having him there had given her life a certain shape: she had shopped for groceries, and made appointments at the dentist. Without Jamie's regular departure for school every day, his irregular arrival from it, Laura's day was huge and formless: meals were pointless, errands could wait. Everything could wait.

"Well, I'm glad he chose Choate. Where else did you look?"

"We looked at Brooks, and Middlesex and Westminster. And St. George's."

"Did you take him around?"

"James and I."

"Both of you?" Laura nodded. "Where was Fox?"

The name.

"I don't know."

Michael raised his eyebrows.

"Well, you know," said Laura, as if this explained everything, "she has a job, and in any case Jamie is not her child. He is James's and my child."

"Very modern," said Michael. "Good for you, going around together."

It had been horrible.

For two days they had driven through New England, the three of them. James and Laura had spoken to Jamie, soliciting his views of each school, discussing the admissions people they had seen, advising him on the interviews. James had spoken seldom to the woman who had been his wife for eight years. His look had been distant and polite: "Would you like more coffee, or shall we go?" he would say. "I'm through, thanks," Laura would answer. The divorce—James's murder of his marriage as Laura saw it—lay before them like a mutilated body, too terrible to mention, too appalling to ignore. Laura had wanted something from James: she was past wanting him back, but she had wanted a sign, a gesture from him, something she could have accepted or rejected, as she wished. But James gave her nothing but courtesy, handing her in and out of the car, holding doors for her, helping her with her coat. He had been courteous five years earlier when he had told her he was leaving her, he had not shouted, or complained, or criticized her.

"Our marriage doesn't work," he had said. "It hasn't worked for years."

But it had worked for Laura, she had been happy married to James. She knew what probably happened on business trips to California, she knew what probably happened during the summer, during the week, while she and Jamie were in the house at the beach, she had accepted that as part of their marriage. It had been worth it: *her* marriage had worked, how could James's marriage have not? But James had been polite and certain. He had pointed out things, the fact that they shared no interests: none. "The fact is," he had said, "that we lead very separate lives. We never talk." But if he had only told her, she would have given up every one of her interests, she would have talked to James without cessation. She would have taken up any interest he had wished. Why had he not told her before that these things, these absurd things, were so important? But James had sighed, and shaken his head. "We are so different," he had said, "it doesn't work." Laura had not understood it at all. "It will be a new chance for us both," James had said. "We will both be released. You can be anything you want to be." But Laura would have none of this. "What I want to be," she had answered, "is a married woman."

James and Laura and Jamie had spent the night in a motel outside of Boston. Laura and Jamie had shared a room, James had had the one next door. After Jamie had gone to sleep Laura had turned off the television and had lain in bed, listening to James's voice in the next room. He had talked to someone for a long time, his voice a steady rhythm in the quiet night. What was he talking about for so long, why did he have so much to say to that person? He had said nothing to Laura all day, nothing really.

When there had finally been silence from James's room, Laura wondered if he was thinking of her on the other side of the wall. She wondered if he ever wanted to tell her anything more, to explain the real reason he had left her, to say something he had not been able to say before. She wondered if he wanted to say kind things about their marriage, if there were any kind thoughts he had about it. She thought of him lying in bed, approaching sleep. She knew how James slept, she knew what shape his body took. She knew how he bent his knees, clasped the edge of the pillow and slept with his chin raised, lifted against the tide of darkness.

"Well," Michael said now, "Sarah took the twins around to look at schools by herself. She was a saint." Sarah was well-known for her saintliness: Michael demanded it. Each year he made his wife drive the children, the dogs and the luggage on the ten-hour trip up to Maine. He flew.

"Have they started to look at colleges yet?" asked Laura, and as Michael answered she wondered suddenly what she looked like. In her wedding pictures, she recognized herself as a pretty woman, with large dark-blue eyes, straight nose, good skin. But since James had left her she had lost her sense of what she looked like, she had lost her own image. She wanted to interrupt Michael, leaning forward to say, "Just tell me, quickly, what I look like. Am I pretty? Am I old? *Can you see me at all?*"

Next to her, Michael stirred in his seat and looked around. They had finished coffee, and Laura wondered if he were getting restless.

"It's a pretty room, don't you think?" she asked. It was high-ceilinged, with carved gilt mirrors and palm trees. She looked around it, but only in one direction. James and the other person were two tables away on her left.

"I think it's a crowded room," said Michael. "Let's go dance."

Laura put her bag on the table and stood up. Michael steered her through the crowd to the tiny dance floor. Dancing with Michael, Laura smiled. She moved her shoulders up and down, and threw her head back: she was having a fine time, a wonderful time. They did funny old-fashioned rock 'n' roll steps, and Laura kept right up with Michael, jigging up and down with the music. She smiled at Michael, and gave a little laugh, to let him know that she was there, that she was alive, and full of whimsy and charm.

The noise was incessant. It was a heavy backdrop of glowering sound, deadening speech, weakening thought. The dance floor was packed, there was really no room to move. Laura could see sweat on Michael's forehead, and her own face was damp, her hair was clinging to it around the edges.

"This is too crowded," yelled Michael, finally, "let's go get a drink."

Laura nodded, and they began to thread their way through the crowd. Laura felt Michael tug at her hand, and turned around. "I'll get my coat," he said, pointing toward the check room, "give me your ticket and I'll get yours." Laura looked surprised, and Michael said, "It's too noisy here. I'll take you home if you'll give me a drink." She nodded, and handed him the ticket from her pocket.

"I'll get my bag," she called, and kept on toward the table. She passed people without speaking. The women smiled at each other and raised their eyes despairingly—it was impossible to speak, the men smiled and shook their heads. She eased in between two tall men, and saw that James and the person were sitting where she and Michael had sat. The woman was in Laura's chair, and next to her was David Ashton, an old friend of James and Laura's. Laura stopped moving.

The woman was talking to David. She was waving her hands and talking very quickly, and David began to laugh. Laura's silver bag was right in front of the woman, on the table. The woman's pale thin arms swooped as she spoke. Laura could not watch her; she could not look away. The two men leaned toward the woman, listening to her. What was she talking about, what on earth was that woman talking about, for such a long time? The two men leaned toward her, smiling.

Laura looked at James. How did he dare talk to David Ashton, who had been in their wedding, who had come to visit them the year they were in South Carolina, who was a part of James and Laura's marriage? How did James dare pretend that he and the other person could be David Ashton's friends? Laura had refused to go to parties where James and the other person would be. She could not tolerate the seepage of new life into old.

James looked up, feeling her eyes on him, and saw Laura. She knew his face, she knew his deep-set eyes, his thick blond eyebrows. James smiled at her, a slow, real smile, his mouth set in kind lines. He was smiling at Laura as he had years ago, when the sight of her was what he wanted.

Surprising herself, Laura smiled back at James. She wondered if he recognized the bag.

The person slapped her hand flat on the table, and began to laugh, both she and David Ashton were laughing, and James's eyes turned from Laura to the woman next to him. David said something, and paused. The woman answered him, shaking her finger at him as though she were in charge of him, as though she were his very good friend. She grinned, and they laughed, all three of them. Without looking behind her, without even glancing to see if it was there, the woman leaned suddenly back against James's shoulder, and was still, smiling at David, the length of her leaning against James's body.

Laura watched them: she felt as though she were stretched out along an enormous high voltage wire, as if wave after wave of shock were flooding through her body. She could not bear it. She wished the woman would stand up and go away, that she would just go away from the silver bag given Laura by her husband. But the woman did not move. She leaned against James, smiling, and James's arm, knowing her, came around her hips, circling her body and holding it next to his.

Laura could not approach them. She took a step forward, but her heart failed her. She could not approach the woman. Laura looked around: she could not go on standing there. Michael was waiting for her. She would leave the bag, and Audrey would find it. Audrey would stay late, after everyone else left, and she would find it and recognize it and take it home. Laura turned around and fled.

In the cab with Michael, watching the darkened streets

go by, Laura wondered if James and the person had seen her leave with Michael. She hoped that they had. She hoped, childishly, that they had felt themselves spurned, that they were staying on a sinking ship by staying on so long in that crowded, earsplitting mass. The real party, the best of it, was over. That was what Laura was signaling by her departure, and she hoped this signal had been seen.

Her apartment was dark and silent: Laura had forgotten Jamie's absence, and had expected to see him, smiling at her from his doorway, looming over her now that he had decided to be a young man. The only light was in her bedroom, revealing the unmade bed, odd shoes lying about the floor, the chaise covered with clothes and books. Laura had tried to be neat when she was married to James: he had hated messiness. Once he had left her she had seen no point in trying; her own eyes did not seem reason enough for that disciplined landscape. She did not choose disorder, nor want it—she was waiting for it to leave her life. It was an interim government.

Laura turned out the light in her bedroom and went into the living room, where Michael was waiting. The paper was spread out on the sofa from last Sunday. She picked it up and carried it into the kitchen, dragging with her toe at a rumpled rug, on the way.

Laura brought in a tray with ice and glasses. In the quiet she could hear the soft rustle of her dress. She put the tray down, and sat next to Michael, on the sofa.

She sighed. "That was a good idea, getting out of there," she said.

"What would you like to drink?" asked Michael. He began opening bottles and clinking ice cubes. Laura watched him, suddenly shy. They were alone.

"How long is Sarah going to be in Santa Barbara?" asked Laura, recalling his marriage to both of them.

"Just till next Wednesday," said Michael.

"Her mother's not sick, is she?"

"Just feeling lonely, between you and me. She's a spoiled old biddy, and she likes to be able to crook her finger and have Sarah come running." Laura did not answer. "I have a question," said Michael.

"Ask."

"Can you put on some music?"

"Yes," said Laura, and got up.

"Put on a dancing record," said Michael, watching her cross the room. "My god," he said, his voice deepened suddenly, an actor's resonance, "My god, woman, there's no reason why we shouldn't dance, just because we're no longer in the middle of a maelstrom." Laura came back to him, smiling, and he stood up. "We have the world before us," Michael said, still booming, and took her in his arms. "There's no reason why we shouldn't dance."

VERTIGO

֍

Michael's affair with Beth had been going on for three years, since 1975. During this time, Michael's wife, Joan, had had a second child and decided to go to medical school. Michael could feel his life settling around him: he had started a family, his wife a career. But nothing had felt settled inside him since the afternoon when, coming back in a taxi from a promotional lunch, he had reached out his hand and traced the line of Beth's smooth white neck, and she had closed her eyes and raised her chin high above his hand, opening her throat to his touch.

Beth was married, too, and at intervals she and Michael would confront each other. One of them would be severe and distant, announcing the end of their affair. The affair did not end.

Beth handled publicity for the books Michael edited. They saw each other daily, and he waited for her to appear in his doorway. In three years he had become brazen. He wrote imaginary names on his calendar: "Baker" scrawled across Thursday afternoon was Beth, in a borrowed apartment, or in a hotel room. Michael met his secretary's eyes easily when he left the office. His voice was firm when he asked for a room at a hotel, no hint of luggage in his hands. Michael sometimes wondered if affairs were like marriages, if in seven years he would become bored with Beth, oppressed by the thought of making love to her. But after three years it seemed there was no end to it.

Standing now in front of his desk, Beth smiled at him. She was pale, though it was midsummer. She had thick red hair, and did not tan. She wore black, a black skirt and a long-sleeved black shirt. The sleeves were rolled up, and showed her long, soft forearms, the skin on the inner sides of them pale and glimmering. The shirt was open at her throat. Her breasts lay just beneath the thin cloth.

"This group is done," Beth said, putting down a file of folders. "This group has problems. When would you like to go over them?"

Her eyes were so clear, so untroubled, that sometimes Michael could not believe that she remembered the subterranean life they shared. It enraged him. She enraged him. He wanted more of her than he could get.

"Right now," said Michael. "Lois, would you mind very much getting us two cups of coffee?"

When the door shut behind his secretary, Michael leaned forward, over his desk, and took Beth's upper arm in his hand. He squeezed it as hard as he could. Beth watched his face intently. She made no sound. She waited for what he would do. Michael would gladly have killed her; his desire felt like rage. He took his hand away but his eyes stayed on her. They watched each other's faces, sunk at once into their secret, all sound from the outside world gone. They were standing like this when Lois returned with the coffee. She must have known; Michael ignored this.

Michael had found them an apartment, belonging to a

friend whose family had moved to the beach for the summer.
That afternoon he took Beth there for the first time. It was
on the Upper West Side: large and dreary, with a faint sour
smell. Coming into the apartment, Beth moved uneasily
through the unfamiliar rooms.

"Are these great friends of yours?" she asked. She was
staring at the wallpaper: blue feathers on a musty tan ground.

"Yeah, great friends," said Michael. "I chose the wallpaper. Come here, would you?"

But Beth drifted farther, inspecting the rooms as if she
were thinking of subletting. Michael waited in the front hall,
impatient. The bedroom was to the left, but Beth vanished
into the string of irrelevant rooms to the right. Michael followed her, pushing open a door and finding himself in the
dining room. It was large and dim, with a battered oak table
and chairs, a dusty rug underfoot. Beth was not in it. Michael
started across the room to the door beyond, and in the quiet
of other people's rooms he found himself walking gently,
almost tiptoeing across the rug. The chairs were pushed un-
tidily in to the table; there was an air of unrest in the room,
of unknown life that went on there. He was an intruder, his
business there was illicit. An uneasy guilt hovered over him,
but he ignored all this, looking for Beth. It was this concentration that had gotten him through the last three years. Like
a tightrope walker he had moved high above the world, above
the shattering flatness that would break him if he fell. He
had not wavered, his eyes fixed on Beth.

In the swinging door that led to the kitchen was a small
glass panel: now, suddenly it framed a face. Sun came into
that corner room, and in the window the face was radiant.
Michael, standing in the dusty shadows of the dining room,
saw the face cut off, lit up, severely framed. The sudden,
silent apparition was unexpectedly frightening: the face was

both strange and familiar to him. In the moment while he stared at it, Michael lost his bearings, his balance. Vertigo overtook him: why was he here, in this strange apartment, in this dim room heavy with other peoples' lives? With horror Michael recognized the face: Joan's. His wife was here. Fear rose in him. He was not ready, his children would be lost to him.

The door swung silently open and he closed his eyes. Beth brushed past him, still remote, preoccupied. He followed her, awash with relief, his balance restored.

Beth found the bedroom and stood still in the center of it. The bed was poorly made, and the nubbly bedspread dragged on the floor. Beth stood with her hands in the pockets of her jacket; she did not look at him. Michael circled her with his arms, breathing in the smell of her. He closed his eyes, sinking. Moving his head slowly, he touched her face with his mouth, not kissing her. "Beth," he whispered, feeling her face with his mouth. "Beth." She did not speak or move, her hands were still in her pockets, but he felt her begin to receive him.

Their love-making mimicked rape. Michael held her hands over her head, his fingers circled her throat. The marks he left on her skin looked painful. He wanted to consume her.

At five o'clock Michael called his office. "Hi," he said to Lois, his voice businesslike. "I'm not going to make it back after all. This thing went on longer than I thought. I'll see you in the morning."

Beth lay naked on the bed beside him. Along the line of her forehead her hair was dark and thick with sweat, her throat was slick with it. He touched her throat and frowned.

"Oh, damn," he said, "I'd forgotten. No, I'll have to come back down for it. That's all right. Thanks, Lois." He hung up. "I forgot a manuscript. There's a meeting on it first thing in the morning. I'll have to go back for it. Want to come? I'll drive you home afterward."

It was a poor offer. It would make Beth late, and for what? They were saturated, they could use no more of each other.

"Yes," Beth said.

They were driven to risks: once Michael, sitting at his desk, had pulled her blouse open across her chest—she was not wearing a bra—and taken her breast in his mouth. No one had come in, but there was no reason for this, it was midmorning.

They took showers, sharing the same soggy orange towel. Beth remade the bed, looping the bedspread again along the floor.

Driving back downtown, Michael asked, "Will this get you in trouble, being late?"

Beth shook her head. "He won't be home until eight."

"What's he up to tonight? His secretary?" Beth's husband was not faithful to her.

She did not look at him. "Tennis lesson," she said.

"Ah, the tennis lesson," said Michael, in his W. C. Fields voice.

"Don't," said Beth.

When they got to the office building, Michael left Beth in the car. "Wait right here," he said, "don't get a ticket." When he came out with the manuscript Beth was in the driver's seat, watching for policemen.

"Get out of there," he said, opening the door. "Next thing you'll want to be on top."

They headed onto the East Side Drive. Once on it, the noise of the traffic became a steady blur, and Beth had to raise her voice to make Michael hear.

"When you were inside, getting the manuscript, I thought, why don't I just leave?"

"And," said Michael, "why didn't you?"

They never used the word love to each other, they never planned anything longer than an afternoon.

Beth leaned her head back against the seat and closed her eyes. "I can't do this anymore," she said, "We have to stop."

Michael drove fast into an emergency pull-off. He slammed on the brakes. They were in a tiny niche off the highway. Iron fencing separated them from the walkway along the East River, which was filled with the spreading, dramatic light of evening. The car stopped so suddenly that Beth was flung forward at the dashboard. She turned to Michael, her eyes alarmed. He opened her blouse, his hands fast and angry. She watched his face. He leaned over and kissed her skin: it was pearl-colored, like the light on the water. On one side of them ran the stream of traffic, swift and constant, on the other was an intermittent pulse of joggers. Beyond them was the steady flood of the river.

Beth closed her eyes. Michael pulled her skirt up to her thighs and put his hand beneath it. What he found was his. His hand insisted, Beth yielded, lying back against the seat, her eyes shut. Neither spoke until Michael said suddenly, desperately, "Get up! Get up!"

He pulled at her blouse, her skirt. In the early summer evening, the lowering sun reflecting itself in the shimmering wash along the river, there was plenty of light for the man leaning in the window to see those parts of Beth that Michael had exposed for himself.

"Need any help?" the man was asking before he had quite seen them, angling his head down into the open window. It was Larry, a salesman from the office.

Michael leaned forward, draping his arms over the steering wheel, trying to shield Beth's painful struggle with her clothes.

"No, thanks," said Michael.

"I thought you were in trouble," Larry said, mortified. "I always stop for a Porsche."

"No," said Michael again, "thanks."

"Well," said Larry, paralyzed, "I'll be on my way."

"Right," said Michael, pushing his chin up into the air, as though this were a kink he could work out. Larry's face, broad, summer-brown, vanished from the window. Michael heard the car start up behind them. It slid past them into the traffic and was gone. Michael and Beth were silent. Beth finished with herself, though she still looked rumpled, not right. Michael put his hand on her hands, lying in her lap.

"I'm sorry," he said gently.

Beth shook her head and smiled at him. "It's all right," she said. It was not, he could see that, and her attempt at reassurance touched him. He pressed her hands.

"Well," he said, but could think of nothing more. She shook her head again. She looked damaged. He started the car and pulled slowly out into the traffic.

They did not speak until they had gotten off the Drive and made their way across town. On a side street near Beth's building Michael stopped the car. By now it was dusk; shadows and darkness were growing in the city from the ground up. Above them the tops of the buildings were still radiant, with a hot sunset light. But their car was already in shadow, and anyone passing would have difficulty seeing them, in the dusk. There was nothing now to see, in any case—they sat far apart, each leaning against a door, as though they had been scalded.

Michael leaned toward her and slid one finger up and down Beth's smooth forearm, but she did not stir.

"Don't feel bad," he said. He would have liked to take her in his arms and blot out that moment, but it had spread, and sunk in.

"It's not that, you know," Beth said, her voice flat. She did not look at him. Michael dreaded what she would say, and took his hand back.

"When I stand outside my door, looking for my keys and wondering if Jack is already home, I want to throw up. I feel like something loathsome. Jack always kisses me hello, and if I've been with you I pull away from him as though I had a disease. I'm terrified he'll be able to tell, just from looking at me. I can't remember how I act normally, what it is that I say when I haven't come home from making love with someone else. What is it normal wives say, people who aren't lying? Sometimes when he makes love to me I start to cry, and I'm terrified he'll notice. I lie still, and lift my chin up so the tears will run into my hair, and not down my cheeks where he'd see them. It seems so terrible to live like this. I think there are only so many things he'll believe, and I don't know how long the list is."

Past them on the sidewalk a woman came by, neat, trim, with high-heeled shoes and carrying a briefcase and a bag of groceries. She walked unhurriedly down the block toward Park.

"I know you're going to say what about Jack's affairs. But it doesn't seem to make any difference to me. I mean about how I behave. I feel as though my life is being poisoned, and I'm the one who's doing it. I can't do it anymore."

They sat without talking in the car, while the street around them darkened. Michael stroked her arm, trying to believe that this was the last time he would do it. When she got out of the car he watched her walk along the sidewalk, trying to memorize her walk, her body. But it looked no different to him. Aside from the sick feeling in the center of him he could not believe anything was different, that there was a reason to memorize anything.

Driving home along the sidling, urgent stream of traffic, the roads slipping in and out of one another, the Major Deegan curving into the Cross County, the Cross County yielding to the Hutchinson, he was aware of himself, inside the tiny, private interior of his car, lit by the intimate lights of the dashboard. Somehow he carried, protected, this frail, small sense of himself, through the strangeness of the rushing world outside, through the shifting, darkening landscape around him.

Larry's face in the window stayed in his mind, sickening. What were the chances of its being someone they knew? But it had been three years. They had used up their odds.

When he got home Joan was at the kitchen table, in front of a pile of catalogues. Neither of them said hello.

"Where are the kids?" asked Michael.

"They've been in bed for hours," Joan said. She did not look up.

"What are all those?" Michael asked, setting down his briefcase.

"Medical schools," said Joan. "I have an interview on Monday in New York, at P and S."

She looked up at him. Michael wondered if he had ever thought her pretty. She had a square, bony face, thick glasses, a solemn mouth. Beth's pale, wistful face appeared in his mind, a painful flash. He wondered how often this would happen.

Joan touched the white streak that flared, illogically— she was only twenty-eight—through her dark hair.

"I'm going to dye my hair," she said tentatively.

"What are you talking about?" Michael asked.

"It makes me look old. They don't want older women."

"You sound like a hooker, for Christ's sake," said Michael. "When you have an interview at Mt. Sinai are you going to have your nose fixed, to look Jewish, or what?" He waited. "That's the stupidest goddamned thing I've ever heard of."

Joan looked away from him, smoothing the streak down. It had been she who suggested, finally, unexpectedly, that they get married. Michael had been ready to give the whole thing up, she had seemed so distant, so unresponsive. They were sitting in a diner in Northampton, late winter, of the year they both graduated, 1970. Michael was stirring his coffee and thinking about the drive back to New Haven, when Joan said, without warning, "Are we going to get married, do you think?" She smiled as she began to speak, then swallowed, and her voice trailed away painfully at the end. Michael looked up and saw that her eyes were full of terror. He had been so touched, by her terror, her awkwardness, her boldness, that he had said, without hesitation, "Yes."

He had thought, after that, things would change between them, that Joan would start to trust him, to unfurl. It had never happened. Joan was still remote, and when the children were born she began to blame Michael for everything. If her car didn't start in the morning she called Michael at his office, not the garage, and if the cat was sick she called Michael, not the vet. If a child was sick she didn't call Michael, in fact she wouldn't speak to him when he came home at night. She seemed to have a mysterious stockpile of resentment, mysteriously growing. Last Christmas her only present to Michael had been a paperback set of Doonesbury cartoons. Not wrapped, it was still in the paper bag from the stationery store.

"Thanks," Michael had said, smiling, holding it up like a prize, "this is great."

"Oh," Joan said vaguely, "I meant to wrap it."

"No, no," said Michael, "it's really great." He turned the book this way and that in the light, as though a certain angle might catch it like a prism, transforming it into something gleaming and wonderful.

He memorized moments like this, he played them over in his mind. Can you blame me? he could ask.

Now, in the kitchen, Michael stared at his wife angrily. "What are you talking about, for Christ's sake?" Joan got up and left the room without speaking. There were now whole groups of days that went by when they did not speak, except in front of the children.

Michael took off his jacket and loosened his tie. The stove was cold, Joan had saved him nothing for dinner. Alone in the dim kitchen he pitied himself. He opened the refrigerator and confronted the sudden flood of cold light and vivid colors: the red and white on the milk carton, the bold blue lettering on the mayonnaise jar, the syrupy red of the ketchup bottle. The brilliant paraphernalia of his family's life, chill and remote to him.

Michael poured himself a glass of milk and sat down at the table, pulling out his manuscript to read. He drank; the milk was sweet and cold in his throat. Admission entered him in a cool, smooth surge like the milk: he was destroying his wife. She could not withstand his anger. The passionate rage Michael felt for Beth he felt too for Joan, but without the desire. And the rage he felt for Joan was pitiless. Her blaming of him was nothing compared to his blaming of her. He set the empty glass down on the table. A thin film of milk colored the inside of it. Tiny air bubbles slid silently down the sides of the glass, gravity asserting itself. Michael thought of the tightrope feeling, the sense of miraculous suspension through belief. He had kept himself up in midair for three years, and Beth, too, just by ignoring everything else, including the laws of physics. It was over, and he felt ashamed, as though he had been behaving like a willful child: pretending there were no such things as laws.

Michael opened the manuscript box and began to read, laying the pages in a neat stack on the table as he finished them. He read carefully, and by the time he was through it was very late.

He pushed his chair farther back and put his head down on the tablecloth. He felt the tablecloth, faintly rough against his cheek, the slight rasp of fine crumbs against his skin. The house was very quiet. He thought of Joan in this house, moving through the rooms when they had first come to look at it. The empty spaces had been alien. Michael had felt nothing for the place; the walls were dirty gray, the wood floors were scratched, and in the children's rooms there were dark squares littering the blank walls, where posters had been Scotch-taped up. He followed Joan from room to room, wondering if they would take the house.

At the window in the upstairs hall she had paused.

"What kind of tree is that?" she asked the real estate agent, turning. Michael had seen her face, the light from the outside falling in a smooth wash, brilliant, fresh, after those gray walls. He had felt delight in her question: it was one he would not have thought of. There were parts of her he did not know, and he sensed her expanding behind him. This will be fun, he had thought.

The agent had told her: cherry. Joan turned to Michael and smiled, faintly. Whatever this was, it was private between them. It will bloom, she had said.

The day it had first bloomed—four years ago—she had called him at the office.

"You should see that tree," she had said.

"What happened?"

"It's a cloud, a white cloud, resting in our garden."

Her voice had been silvery, excited. Michael had smiled into the telephone.

"Good," he said. "Great!"

Now he turned his head on the table, propping his cheek on his forearm. He was too tired to get up. He opened his eyes and looked around the dim kitchen. The change of angle made the room disorienting, askew. He remembered the time he had had an inner ear infection, and Joan had driven him to the doctor's office early on Saturday morning. He didn't dare drive himself, his balance was gone.

Walking across the parking lot, the mist rising in steamy clouds from the blacktop, the trees cold and dripping, Michael had felt the ground tip smoothly beneath him, his feet had jarred unexpectedly, horridly, against the pavement. He stopped, tipping. Anything might come next to him, anything at all: cosmic night.

What had actually happened was that Joan, without speaking, had put her hand with great conviction around his elbow, her other arm across the small of his back. She had walked the rest of the way across the parking lot with her body pressed against his, making her balance his, holding him in a gravity he could trust. He had not realized that she was so tall, as tall as he, almost. And strong: he had not realized that she could support him.

Michael stood up slowly at the table, pushing his chair gently back. He leaned over the table, his head down, his weight propped on his knuckles for a moment before he straightened. He stood still, feeling the house quiet around him, the night outside the black windows. The noises in the kitchen intensified: the hum of the refrigerator, and the beat-pause of the clock. He stayed motionless at the table—what was he waiting for? He thought he felt himself swaying slightly, but could not tell. He could not tell if it was the solitude, the hum of silence, deepening in his head, the black shadow, the lateness of the hour.

He concentrated, willing himself out of his dim hypnotic state. He stared at the windowsill above the counter, focusing hard, daring it to tilt. On it, in measured placement, were the four hand-painted mugs: Michael and Joan on the ends, Mark and Kate in between. Michael narrowed his eyes at the mugs, focusing hard, trying to tell whether or not he was swaying, whether or not he was solid. He willed himself to be solid.

As he left the kitchen, Michael turned out the light, and, as he moved through the house toward Joan, he darkened each room as he passed through it.

DAUGHTER

❧

I wake up. I am a coward, so I pretend that this has not happened, and I do not move. I lie with my eyes shut, listening to my husband getting dressed, down the hall. He returns, after a while, dressed. He kisses me good-bye. I feign somnolence. He strokes me, and I move sleepily, hoping this will produce more stroking, but he is armed against the day: shaved, brushed, and neat, a timetable in his brief-case, he is proof against my groggy charms. He kisses me again and leaves; I hear the car going down the driveway.

It is now seven-fifteen, and I should wake up my daughter. If I do not wake her soon, we will have to race in order to make the school bus at eight o'clock. My daughter hates this. So do I. I also hate to wake her up. She has lavender shadows under her eyes; she has not been getting enough sleep. She is almost six, and needs at least eleven hours. These first few weeks of school have been difficult; I cannot seem to get her to bed early enough, bathed, read to, body clean and mind calm by seven-thirty. This is, of course, my fault, which makes me irritable and defensive.

I lie in bed now, hoping that she will wake up by herself.

Soon she does. I hear her bare feet padding across the floor. She comes into my room like a sleepwalker, her eyes heavy, face rumpled, mouth working like a nursing infant's. She climbs into bed and burrows into me, her eyes closed in bliss. "I love you," she says, "You're so warm."

It is true, I am warm. I am sheathed in warmth, in the cocoon woven by my husband and me, by our bodies as we slept. I wrap myself around her. For this while, the two of us entwined and breathing, I supply my daughter effortlessly with all she needs. It is miraculous. I smooth her soft back beneath the covers: what I am now is just exactly what she wants.

It is now seven-thirty, reluctant as I am to acknowledge this. I nudge my daughter; she resists. It is hard to dismantle the scene. Looking again at the clock, I become alarmed, urgent. I get up, pull on my blue jeans, turtleneck sweater. I take her into her room to get dressed. I am sharp and insistent now. I am afraid of missing the bus, an event I treat as I would the eruption of Vesuvius. I wait impatiently as she stands at her closet door, considering her clothes. Seconds go by. She is immobile. I complain. She pulls out a dress that she knows is much too big for her, a present from an older cousin. She glances defiantly at me as she holds it up: my sharpness has elicited a response. We are not identical, my daughter and I, but we echo each other's shapes. I am the material from which she was cut; we twist and curl, toward and away from each other, required by some law of emotional physics to react forever to each other's acts.

I appear to be a kind and generous mother. I am profligate with my affection, extravagant with my love for my daughter. I read to her for hours, I give her milk and graham crackers after school, we have long talks, expeditions, but she and I know the intensity of the demands I make on her.

I want her simply perfect: modeled after me but without my flaws. I teach her patience, though I myself do not approach it; I tell her to be kind, though she is the most frequent recipient of my own unkindnesses. I want her to share my tastes. I want her to choose books over television, wheat bread over Fritos, English sandals over ripple-soled wedgies. She loves me, and it does not occur to her that my demands might be unreasonable. She does her best to please me, and though this does, of course, please me, it frightens me as well.

She resists me on some things, however, for which I am grateful. Her taste in clothes, for example, is entirely her own. She likes gowns, ruffles, tiny waists, and swirly skirts. She is appalled by my loose tunics, tight blue jeans, leather boots. She tells me gently that I would look much nicer if I tucked my shirt in.

We reach an agreement on her clothes and go downstairs. I am carrying her shoes and socks. "You put these on while I make your breakfast," I say, knowing she will not. I give my daughter her vitamin, the dog his heartworm pill. I slice bread, make toast, scramble eggs, pour milk. It is now quarter to eight. By the time her breakfast is ready, my daughter has not yet swallowed her vitamin pill. Watching the clock, I am becoming frantic. I say angrily, of the pill, "Oh, for *good*ness' sake," and my daughter's face darkens. She says, *"Okay, Mommy!"* and takes the pill. I relent consciously, and pat her tensely on the head. I carry her food into the breakfast room, which reproaches me with its clutter. The laundry basket takes up most of the tiny table, dead leaves lie scattered under all the plants. While she eats, I brush my daughter's hair, and talk to her about school. My daughter is new there, and she is having trouble settling down. She is a discipline problem at school, although not at home. I begin braiding the fine blond hair; she is a beautiful child, with smoky eyes and long lashes.

I talk to her about rules. I explain why they exist, how we all have to obey rules.

I sound reasonable, but this is deceitful, for I am not addressing the problem, which is her own insecurity in new surroundings, not the notion of discipline, which is one she is perfectly comfortable with. I am using rhetoric her five-year-old mind cannot refute, but she senses my purpose. "I don't like to hear what you're saying—you sound as if you're *making* me obey, not *helping* me obey," she says precociously. I soften, caught, but I cannot give in. She may defy me, she may have tantrums in front of me, but before strangers I want her perfect. Is it for me or for herself that I want this perfection, do I want admiration of something for itself, or do I want reflected pride in the creation of such an object? Probably both. At any rate, I am frantic at the thought of her deliberate disobedience at school, and I want to quell it. I tell her I am sorry to sound as if I am trying to *make* her obey (though she is right) but that I don't know any other way to talk about the rules. (What I want is for her teachers to love her as I do. It is mystifying to me that they do not. Loved, my daughter is radiant, ingenuous, responsive.)

I go on disingenuously about obeying rules, but she is no longer listening. "Where are my library books?" she asks. Miraculously, I know. "I'll get them, it's time to go." It is now seven minutes to eight. I get the books, and her jacket. "Come on," I say urgently. "We'll miss the bus." "Wait a minute," my daughter calls. "I have to put on my shoes and socks."

I am furious. We *will* miss the bus. Why did I not wake her up earlier? "Oh, for *good*ness' sake," I say, viciously, as though she has broken something precious. She comes out of the breakfast room, laughing. Her shoes and socks are on, buckled. "I was only teasing," she says, picking up her library books. I laugh loudly and quickly, to cover up for my first reaction, which shames me. "You are a teaser," I say, giving her power over me. "You always trick your mommy." She smiles, pleased.

In the car, on the short trip to the bus stop, we discuss her birthday. She wants spaghetti for dinner, she says firmly, and she goes on to tell me what she plans to wear to her party. It is her ugliest dress, a faded hand-me-down, too long, draggled and unbecoming. She loves it because it has a full skirt, which twirls gratifyingly, and white ruffles at the neck and cuffs. Her grandmother made a lacy pink one that looks enchanting on her; nonetheless, I hold my tongue, virtuously conscious of my largeness of spirit: it is my daughter's body, her party.

We arrive at the bus stop. We have not missed the bus; the eighth grader who lives there is standing in the driveway, swinging her book bag from side to side. She comes over, as she does each morning, to open the door for my daughter. I am relieved of tension, filled with love, with repentance. I want my daughter to spend her day wrapped and protected by my love, as she was earlier wrapped and protected by my body. "You look lovely in your new jacket," I say, of an early birthday present. "I hope you have a good day at school. Can I have a hug?" She leans toward me across the seat, her face radiant, empty of resentment at the morning's unfairnesses. Her body curves obligingly into a backward half-moon as I hug her fiercely. She pulls away, smiling, conscious of the eighth grader's hand on the door handle. "I love you," I say, wanting to erase the roughness of the morning. My daughter nods. "I love you," she says kindly, but her attention has gone. The eighth grader opens the door, and my daughter climbs out of the car, showing off her new jacket. I wait for a moment in the car, but my daughter does not look at me again. She is talking to the older girl, and scuffing at the stones in the driveway with her English sandals. I am pleased to see her scuffing them. Perhaps she will escape me after all.

HANDICAPPED

Mother calls me twice a year, once before Thanksgiving and once before Easter.

"Hello, James? It's your mother." This was the before-Easter call. She is not, of course, my mother, but I am used to the word: it's what I have called her since I was five.

"Hello, Mother," I said.

"How are you, dear, and Cynthia?" she asked. This is form.

"We're fine; how are you and Dad?"

"We're just fine. Though I'm a little worried about your father. He's been a little short of breath lately."

I don't know my father very well, so I ask about him as though he were a relative of hers, as though my primary concern is her anxiety. How long has this been going on, I asked, has he seen a doctor, what does the doctor say?

"About a month, I think. He first mentioned it to me in the beginning of February. A kind of tightness, he said, a compression in his chest. When he mentioned it a second time I took him right away to the doctor. Our nice Dr. McCormack thought we should see a specialist."

"And what did the specialist say?"

"They told your father to eat more fresh vegetables and less salt, and not to run upstairs two steps at a time." Mother gives a little bark of laughter. She talks quickly and intensely; she is an energetic woman.

"What does Daddy say?" My father never runs anywhere. His exercise is golf.

"He's offended. He says he's not a handicapped person, and he won't be treated like one. He says he doesn't want me putting in *ramps* all over the house." She waited for me to laugh, which I did. By making my father sound crusty and independent, Mother made herself sound twinkly, soft-hearted, and ineffectual.

"Well, Mother, it sounds as though you've done everything that could be done. Keep me posted, though."

She ignored the last. "I hope I have," she says, "I hope I have." She turned brisker. "Now: Easter. I'm expecting you at quarter to one, is that all right? We'll have the egg hunt before lunch, and we'll sit down at one-fifteen."

At Thanksgiving my stepbrothers come, John and Hugh, and my stepsister, Angela, and their spouses and children. Usually some of them turn up at Easter, but this year it was just Cynthia, me, and our two children. My father and Mother still live in the big stone house in Greenwich where I grew up, though they have been talking, recently, about selling the main house and moving into the gate house. John, Hugh, and Angela are against this, but it wouldn't bother me at all. Stone houses are always cold. Step inside that big, square front hall, even in the summer, and the chill enters right into you.

My daughters, Kate and Annie, call the house a castle. It does look like one: high, slate-roofed, with a round turret at one end, and the huge topiary flanking the driveway. They think it's like the castle in Cinderella, and in a way it is. They wish we went there more often, but we go only twice a year, though it's only half an hour from where we live.

My mother left my father and me when I was five years old. I don't remember her leaving, but I remember first arriving at the stone house.

My father stopped the car in the portico and we got out, crunching loudly on the gravel. The house seemed very large and gloomy, and as we walked into the cold front hall it felt like a cave. There were no rugs in it yet, and it was dark. I looked around, and the woman my father had married leaned over to unbutton my coat for me.

I stood still and looked straight up over my head, at the plaster ceiling with its dim complicated patterns. For some reason this frightened me: I had never seen a ceiling with designs on it. Walls had decorations on them, ceilings were plain. I felt disoriented. With my head tilted back, staring up at the patterns, I felt as though the floor might tip up at any minute, the world might be entirely dislocated.

"Now, James," said the woman. She had knelt down in front of me, and I could smell her—her skin, the faint sharpness of her breath, her strange perfume. I could see the separate eyelashes, coming out of reddish openings, I could see the tiny duct in the inner corner of her eye, the taut, polished skin on her nose. She was smiling, and seemed to have too many teeth.

"James, dear, you know you have come to live here with us, now. You are going to stay here in this house, with your father and me, and John and Hugh and Angela. From now on you are only going to see your mother for a month, each summer. I am going to be your real mother now, so I want you to call me Mother. You are to call her Aunt Emily."

She was kneeling in front of me, and had both her hands on the lapels of my coat; my small chest was rising and falling beneath her palms. I was five years old. I gazed at her. I had been told about the visit to my mother, one month a year. I didn't understand it; it didn't seem possible to me. I didn't think in terms of months or years, only in terms of days. But each day passed and she was not in it. I could see that everything would be strange from now on.

I looked at my father. His back was to me and he was hanging up his coat. I waited to see if he would turn and say something about this, but he didn't. When he had put his coat away he walked away from both of us—me and this strange, too close woman who had fixed me with her eyes, her hands gripping my coat. When he had gone into the living room, out of earshot, she spoke again.

"I want you to say it, James," she said, not releasing my coat. "Call me 'Mother.' "

I waited, still, but my father didn't come back, and my mother had somehow been taken out of my life. I seemed to have no choice. I answered her. "Mother," I said.

"That's right," she said, and she smiled into my face. I could feel my heart pounding in my chest, beneath her big hands.

On the drive over, at Easter, Kate and Annie were full of excitement. They were dressed up in freshly ironed, puffy-skirted Easter dresses, with those flat-soled shiny black shoes, and flimsy, short white socks. Their clean, silky hair was flyaway, and Cynthia took out her hairbrush just before we turned into the driveway.

"Now remember," Cynthia said, smoothing Annie's head, "remember that when you shake hands hello, you look people straight in the eye. And you can give Grandfather and Grandmother a kiss if you like. And remember to say 'please' and 'thank you,' and not to interrupt when grown-ups are having a conversation." The girls' faces turned up to her like flowers, absorbed, as though she were teaching them a new language.

When we arrived, Mother came out into the big dark hall, her heels clicking on the stone flags, silent on the heavy carpets. Mother is a small, neat woman, with wiry, lusterless blond hair, a short, straight nose and faded blue eyes. She is slightly stooped, at sixty-eight, but trim. She was wearing two beige cashmere sweaters, one on top of the other, the way women do, and gold earrings and her pearls.

"Hello, dears!" she said.

"Hello, Mother." I leaned over and she gave me a strong little hug and an air kiss right next to my cheek. She has been kissing me like that for thirty-five years.

"Hello, Cynthia, dear!" She gave Cynthia the same. Kate and Annie waited, suddenly bashful in their fancy clothes, trying to remember, exactly, what it was they were meant to do.

"And hello, Annie. Hello, Kate." Mother leaned down and held out her hand. Annie, who is four, stepped forward, boldly seized Mother's hand in both of hers, and kissed it. Cynthia and I both laughed, and then Cynthia said gently, "Not on her hand, sweetie. You can give Grandmother a kiss on her cheek." Stricken, Annie looked up, paralyzed with shame.

Mother's face did not change. She waited, bent over, hand outstretched, for Annie to recover. When Annie didn't move, Mother blinked impatiently and turned to Kate.

"Hello, dear," Mother said to Kate.

Annie's eyes began to fill, and Cynthia held out her hand. Annie took it and buried her face in Cynthia's skirt, mortified.

Kate stepped forward and took Mother's hand politely, shook it, and reached up to give Mother a soft little kiss on the cheek.

"Why thank you, Kate," Mother said. "How nice. Now let's go in and see your grandfather." With Kate's hand still in hers, Mother turned her back on Annie, who gave a huge sob against Cynthia's thigh. Cynthia picked Annie up and began to whisper in her ear.

My father was sitting in the living room, his drink on the table beside him. The living room is formal, with French furniture, Belgian tapestries on the wall, and tall French windows giving out onto the lawn. The library, which is mostly English, is cozier. But it was Easter, so we were in the living room. My father didn't stand, but he raised his hand in greeting.

"Well, well, well," he said, smiling his party smile, swinging his foot gaily. "Look who's here."

"Here's Kate," said Mother, leading Kate over to him. Kate held Mother's hand, docilely waiting to be presented. Her silky hair looked polished, and her short skirt hovered over her silvery-pink legs. The fresh bloom of her skin was astonishing against the faded colors and the heavy quiet of the room.

"Hello, Grandfather," Kate said politely, holding out her hand. My father held out his hand. He is seventy-two, quite hale, with a long face and pink cheeks. He still has all his hair, though it is tame now, and slopes meekly against his skull. His eyebrows, in contrast, are vigorous: bristly and wild. He wears colorless glasses, tweed jackets, and pants in luscious shades. That day he was dressed up for Easter, in a blue blazer and sober gray flannel pants.

My father was leaning away from Kate, his spine set firmly against the chair's back, his legs crossed at the knee.

A kiss would have been difficult; he and Kate shook hands.

"Hello, Miss Kate," he said, "Happy Easter."

Mother turned around. "Where has Annie got to?" she asked. Cynthia had followed us, and was standing serenely behind us. Annie was in her arms, mostly recovered.

"Here's Annie," Cynthia said, and my father waved at her.

"Hello, Annie," he said, "Happy Easter."

Later there would be Easter baskets, but for now the children's time was over. We sat down in the handsome French chairs, and the maid brought us drinks. The girls got their favorites—ginger ale with cherries in them—and they sipped these as they leaned against our legs, bored, languid, half-listening to our conversation.

"Well, John called last night," Mother said.

"How is he?" I asked.

So we heard all about John and Ellen: whether or not John should have been offered a partnership, whether Ellen sends the children to play groups too early, whether their apartment in Chicago is big enough for them. They live very comfortably. After he married Mother, my father very generously arranged things so that my step-siblings have inherited his father's money, at least the part that he controlled. My father explained to me once that he had done this in order to be fair. I was meant to inherit money from my mother's side of the family, to make up for the loss to me. As it turned out, though, this never did happen; there was a problem with the trusts, and all of it went to my two sisters, who lived with my real mother.

When we had finished with John, my father cleared his throat and looked at me. "You know, that Alex Wagner gave me the most amazing stock to buy," he said, giving his broad social smile and shaking his head in admiration. "The guy just doesn't seem to make a false move."

"Oh, really?" I said. "What did he give you?" I manage money myself.

"He called me up—and you know he rarely does that, it's only if it's really important—and told me about a company that he said I just shouldn't miss. He really *insisted* that I buy it. So I did. Now, that was six months ago, and I'll be doggoned if it hasn't doubled." My father smiled and shook his head, pleased and admiring, swinging his foot, in its polished loafer, up and down.

"What was the stock?" I asked again.

Now my father's tone changed, his voice turned loud and professional. "A little company called Radco," my father said, frowning faintly. "I doubt if you'd even have heard of it. Just a little company he got hold of, and —" he shook his head again—"I don't know how he does it." He brightened, and his voice turned social again. "But I'm glad he does— now your Mother and I are rich!" He laughed: a joke.

"Radco," I said, "is the company I told you to buy a year ago."

My father looked at his glass and took a drink from it. He gave a faint, residual shake of his head.

"I told you to buy that company a year ago," I repeated. "It was at three when I told you about it."

My father looked at Mother and smiled. "Couldn't have been the same company."

"There is only one company called Radco," I said, "and that's the one I told you to buy."

My father, still looking at Mother, waved his hand. "You have so many different stocks, I can't keep them all straight." He looked at me and smiled engagingly, ingenuously. "And

I'm never sure exactly what it is you do with them. I mean what it is exactly that you do."

I went to Harvard Law, as my father did, and afterward I practiced as a lawyer, as he did, but only for four years. It has been nine years since I left the law to manage mutual funds, which I have done ever since. What it is, exactly, that I do, is manage people's money, though not my father's.

"I manage people's money," I said. "I've been doing it for nine years."

My father smiled at Mother and shook his head. "Always chopping and changing, I can't keep track." He laughed.

"Nine years," I said.

My father waved his hand in the air toward me. "Oh, all right," he said dismissively. "Anyway," he went on, changing his tone, and using the word as if it were an explanation, or a reply, or the start of a new conversation, "an-y-way . . ." My father smiled at Kate.

There was a pause, and then Mother turned to the girls. "Well, now, Kate and Annie. What about the Easter bunny? Shall we go and see if he's been here? In the library? I have a feeling we should look in the library."

At two o'clock the next morning I slowly discovered myself awake in the dark. There I found myself: lying beside Cynthia and staring at the black ceiling. There was a noise in the silence of our bedroom, and I thought that was what had woken me up. It was a while before I could identify it. The room was completely black, and it was soundless except for this slow, even, granite rumble. It seemed like something from inside the earth, distant, inexorable. I lay there for what seemed a long time listening and wondering before I recognized it: my teeth, grinding away on their own.

It seemed they were grinding to a slow rhythm of words,

like wheels on a train. *What-it-is-exactly-that-you-do*, they were saying. It took a while for me to realize this, and as I did I discovered that my whole body was suffused with rage. My hands were clenched, my chin was raised and tight. For a long while I lay there, bathed in rage. I felt helpless in its grip. Driving home in the car I had angrily asked Cynthia, "Why does he do it? Why does he act like that?" I meant the question to be rhetorical, but she answered. "Your father can't help it. Think of him as handicapped."

I didn't like hearing that. I snapped at Cynthia and the conversation had ended. I refused to think of my father that way. But lying in the dark in the middle of the night there is nothing else to do besides think, and I began to wonder why I was so determined not to see my father that way. Part of me wanted to lie there, clenched, for the rest of my life. But there was something else, some other emotion which I couldn't identify, quite strong, that wanted me to move, to change. Part of my brain seemed quite disinterested, and floating free from the anxiety and anger that held my body. And though I didn't want to risk any change, which was frightening, in the dark, alone, it seemed safe at least to explore these things, slowly, carefully. It was all private, I wouldn't have to admit to anything, later.

What if I did think of my father that way—weak? And I could see that, for one thing, it would mean giving up my rage, and the disconnected part of my mind saw that I didn't want to do that. There was something sweet and comforting about my rage: it was familiar, and it made me feel powerful and independent. And lying there, I was modestly impressed that I had all this energy at hand, this dark strength that had set my jaw into such deep and satisfying action.

I often asked myself why my father behaved the way he did toward me. Asking it made me angry and powerful, and the question itself made me important, into my father's equal, an adversary. Now, to erase Cynthia's response I answered it myself, to hear the answer I wanted. He does it because he hates me, was the answer, and it made me feel bold and triumphant. My rage was vindicated. I whispered it in the darkened room: "My father hates me." I had never heard it said before, but it didn't do what I had hoped. Hearing the spoken words made me feel somehow diminished, even ashamed. What I was saying seemed boastful and false, because I knew it wasn't true. My father doesn't hate me.

My real mother came once to the stone house. I was eight years old. My two younger sisters, who lived with my mother, spent a month in the summer with my father, just as I spent a month with my mother. The time my mother came was to bring my sisters for their month. They didn't often come when I was there. Sometimes I was at camp, sometimes I was at my mother's, but this time they came to the stone house while I was in it. And this one time, for some reason, it was my mother who brought them.

I don't know who told me my mother was coming to the stone house—maybe Ilonia, the woman who looked after me. But I remember standing in the front hall, waiting for her. I remember staring out the leaded window beside the wide heavy front door, watching the empty driveway. I leaned against the glass and stared. I kept imagining my mother's car appearing between the big, shaped yew trees. I told myself the car would be there when I counted to twenty, and I counted to twenty. I told myself the car would be there when I counted to fifty. I moved to the other side of the door, and I looked out of that window, my cheek pressed against the pane. I told myself the car would be there when I counted to twenty.

I heard Mother tiptap into the hall, and I shrank away from the window. I wasn't doing anything wrong, but as soon as I heard her I wished I had heard her earlier and had slid into the cloakroom, out of sight. But she had been silent on the big thick carpets, and now she had seen me. She came up behind me and put one hand on my shoulder.

"James," she said.

"Mm," I said.

"Answer me properly, James."

"Yes, Mother."

She knelt down in front of me so I could see her huge face.

"Now, James, your Aunt Emily is bringing your sisters here for their visit today, you know that."

I nodded.

"But you know this isn't your time to see your Aunt Emily."

I didn't say anything.

"You know you see Aunt Emily in August, when you go to her house. This is just an accident, her coming here with your sisters." She waited. I was looking past the gold fuzz of her hair, out the small leaded windowpanes. I was thinking, if the car comes now, if it comes right now. "So I want you to go upstairs and wait for your sisters up there. You'll see them when they come. But it's not your time to see your Aunt Emily."

I looked back at Mother. Her eyes were right there, she was staring into me, waiting.

Here is how I had thought it would happen: I had thought I would stand next to the door until my mother's car pulled up on the loud crackle of our driveway, her old green car in front of the stone house—not an accident, a miracle—and she would get out of the car, with her beautiful reddish hair loose on her shoulders, smiling when she saw me. I would have gone over to her, across the crunchy gravel, and she would have put her arms around me, all the way around me. She would have knelt, easily, as she always did, and put her arms around me, as she always did, so that my whole body was held against her whole body, and so that my head leaned against hers, and I could smell the warm smell of her hair.

"Do you understand, James?" Mother said, her eyes fixed on mine. "This is not your time to see her. I want you to go upstairs to your room, dear." Then, since I didn't move right away, she said warningly, "Right now."

My bedroom was up on the third floor. My window looked out the back of the house, over the broad green lawn toward the sound. I sat in the chair beside my window and waited there. It was completely quiet up there. I felt a terrible tightness in my chest, a pain, and then a drawing-in noise startled me. I realized that I was crying.

Now, lying in the dark, I wondered where my father had been that day, as my beautiful mother with her reddish-brown hair approached the stone house. It had been she who had left my father, it was he who had been abandoned. I thought now of how that would be, how it would be if Cynthia left me: your connection with the rest of the world, your life, abruptly cut off. There you would be, alone on a small perilous piece of land, with swift dangerous currents rushing around you, deep water between you and the world—you would wonder if a rescue party, an explorer, might ever appear. You would have to make your life up, step by step, not knowing how to make it work. My father couldn't manage on his own, he never had: he saw himself as helpless. And I wondered if he had been sitting in one of the upstairs rooms facing the sound, listening for the wheels on the gravel.

I thought of the three of us, my father, my stepmother, and I, arriving for the first time at the stone house, all of us anxious about this shared life. Me numb and passive, waiting only to see my real mother; my father dull and shamed, waiting to see if his new wife would leave him, too. Mother vibrating with tension, afraid she could not dispel the presence of the woman who had so unmanned both my father and me. I thought of my father standing in the front hall and hearing this new wife tell me to call her Mother. It is women who run our lives, and my father, like me, had had no choice. He had handed himself over to Mother like a prisoner, hoping she would be merciful. It was an unconditional surrender, and I was part of the settlement.

I lay in that silence, in that blackness. My own wife slept next to me, sharing the air I breathed; her generous body warmed mine. She had not left me. I was so grateful to my wife for not leaving me. I was so grateful to her for loving my children. I felt as though I would never be able to repay her for this. My whole body ached in gratitude, I wanted to wake her up and thank her.

It was by then the depths of the night, the very bottom. There was no hope of dawn, or distraction, anything but these thoughts. Finally I thought of what I could no longer avoid: of my father's meek hair, the anxious lines around his mouth. His party smile, his nervous feet in their polished loafers. Seeing him in this way was terrible, and I could see—I must have known it all along, just as I had known that he did not hate me—that Cynthia had been right. My father was an accident victim, he radiated fear and damage. He had an invisible limp, he had that wary caution in his eyes that handicapped people have, the fear of a pain too intimate and well known ever to discuss. He had been like this always, all the time I had known him.

I didn't want to know my father weak, I didn't want to see him frightened. I didn't want to hear about pains in his chest. I wasn't ready, and it spoiled my rage. But I could feel my rage losing its comfort, it was going, somehow, dissolving in the silence and the dark, giving way to something else, the second feeling behind all this.

And I lay there in the dark, with that terrible knowledge, which was my love for my father, flooding through me, making me ache. And I wished that my father's handicap had been physical. There are things you can do for physical handicaps. I could have been doing them for years: helping him down the stairs, lifting him from his chair. I could have put a spoon gently in his mouth, fed him. Eased the pains in his chest.

TEARS BEFORE BEDTIME

Eldon left for a business trip on Sunday afternoon, and got back on Thursday. He was supposed to come home early that night so he could see the girls before we went out to dinner, but something must have come up, and on Thursday afternoon he called to say he would be late. I wasn't surprised.

I got home around six, and Flora, our housekeeper, gave me Eldon's message. "Thank you, Flora," I said. Flora is Filipino, small and slight, and her expression never changes. Sometimes I wonder if she thinks all American marriages are like this. I wonder if she feels sorry for me when she tells me, again, that my husband isn't coming home. "Oh, that's fine," I say to Flora. I act very businesslike, to make it clear that it's normal, that I don't feel angry or abandoned, that this is what American marriages are like. For all I know, it is what Filipino marriages are like: the wife living her own life alone with her children, the husband absent.

I had spent the afternoon at a board meeting downtown, for the women's shelter. We argued for three hours over how to spend the city money we had just received. Some people thought we should start to expand our program and hire more staff. I think the money should go straight into the shelter itself. We've just started it up, and the rooms are horrible. The paint is peeling, the floors are splintery, and there is no furniture. The women sit on mattresses on the floor, one light bulb in the ceiling overhead, little cooking rings plugged into the wall, with their silent children around them. It's better than the street, but it's still horrible. Staff expansion: it made me angry.

I told Flora that I would make supper for the girls, since I hadn't seen them all day. Alice set the table. She is six, and looks just like her father, with his long chin and dark blue eyes. After she set the table she came back into the kitchen. Sarah, who is four, was kneeling on a chair, drying the lettuce with a paper towel. Alice leaned against Sarah, who ignored her.

"Alice," I said, to distract her. "Did you finish with the table?"

"I couldn't," said Alice. "There aren't any glasses." She bumped Sarah's arm, and Sarah pulled her arm away and glared at her sister.

"Stop that," Sarah said.

"I didn't do *anything*," Alice said scornfully.

"You bumped my arm," Sarah said.

"There aren't any glasses," I said. "Isn't that strange. Do you think someone came into the kitchen and stole the glasses? Or what could have happened to them since lunch?" I looked at Alice.

"Well, there aren't any," Alice said.

"You mean there aren't any in the cupboard," I said. "Did you look in the dishwasher?" Alice glanced up at me and then back at Sarah. Sarah had covered the lettuce with the damp towel, and was gently patting it in circles. I knew what she was doing: she was putting the lettuce to sleep. This is how she sees the world. Her feet are named Jane and Mary, and when we put on her boots, first we put on Jane boot, then Mary boot. The next time we put on Mary boot first, to be fair.

Alice was standing on the outer edge of one foot, balancing her weight on it and tottering back and forth. Now she tipped into Sarah, hard, bumping her arm again, interrupting the slow incantatory motion.

Sarah gave a shrill cry. "*Stop* that, Alice! Now you've ruined *everything*."

"Oh, I have not ruined *everything*," Alice said, disgusted, but in a low voice, glancing up at me sideways to see if she was in trouble. She moved a step back from Sarah, to strengthen her position. I met her cautious eye with a hard one, and she made a scornful sound and yanked herself away, over to the dishwasher, to see if it held the disappearing glasses. They were there, miraculously enough, and clean. Alice reluctantly took out two, holding one in each hand sloppily, and began dragging herself across the floor.

"Don't drop those," I said warningly.

"I *won't*," said Alice, and as I turned back to the hamburgers she stuck her tongue out at Sarah, who had looked up to see what Alice was not to drop. Energetically and at once Sarah stuck out her own tongue, all the way to the roots, squeezing her eyes shut, and frowning wildly, her hands on her hips, enraged.

When Sarah had finished her dinner I declared the meal over. Alice's plate was still full of mess—pale hamburger bloodied with ketchup, bits of lettuce, and lima beans that had been bloodied, too. In the kitchen I took her plate and scraped everything into the garbage, with quick, brisk strokes. I hate leftovers.

After we had cleaned up from dinner I told the girls they could play for half an hour, until bedtime. They followed me into my bedroom while I started running the tub. Alice started whining about television.

"Why can't I watch it?" she said, "Only for one show."

"Because you can't, that's the rule," I said. "Not during the week."

"But whyyy?" asked Alice, her voice high, dragging out the word like a fingernail on the blackboard. I didn't answer. "Why?" she said again, and again, and again. Sarah was sitting on my bed, dressing one of her dolls, and talking to it quietly.

Eldon thinks they should be allowed to watch television. All their friends do, he says. We're cutting them off from the rest of the world, he says. I think letting children watch television is like feeding horses straw: you kill their appetites for real food by stuffing them with trash. I'd be happy if we didn't even own a television, but Eldon likes to watch tennis matches and football games on it. Alice comes and hangs over his shoulder, leaning heavily against him.

"That was a good shot, wasn't it, Daddy," she says hopefully.

"It sure was," Eldon says.

"I could see it was a good shot," Alice says. "He's going to cream Lendl, isn't he?" If Eldon doesn't answer she pushes at him, joggling at his shoulder until he responds.

"I guess so," Eldon says, his eyes on the television.

"I hate Lendl, don't you?" she says.

But this is wrong.

"No, I don't hate Lendl," Eldon says, turning to her. He reaches up over his shoulder and takes her by her plump arms. "Why do you hate Lendl, Alice?" His voice is careful and concerned. He waits for a moment and repeats, like a moderator, "Why do you hate Lendl, Alice? What makes you say that?"

But Alice retreats from him, slapping at his hands. She won't answer. This was not what she had planned. She hangs away, behind her father, until he turns back again to the tennis match on television.

Now, Alice was exasperated by my silence. I had undressed and was just getting into the tub when she said, "Daddy would let us watch TV if he were here." She said it sulkily, her head ducked, peering up at me beneath her bangs.

I turned around. "Out," I said, pointing to the door of my room.

"All right," said Alice, crossly taking it back, "I won't watch TV." But I had had enough.

"Out," I said again, "I mean it." When she didn't move I slammed over to my closet and pulled on my bathrobe. I went out into the hall and called for Flora.

"Mommy, I *won't* watch TV," said Alice, alarmed. "I don't even care about it," she lied. But it was too late. Flora came and took her by the wrist, and they went off to the girls' bedroom, Alice wailing. I won't have this emotional blackmail.

Sarah sat on my bed, watching Alice being taken away, her eyes solemn. "You're a bad girl," she whispered to her doll, "a very bad girl to do that."

When Eldon came home I was dressed and ready. He went in to say good night to the girls, and sat down on Alice's bed. I was walking past the door and I heard Alice say to him, aggrieved, in a half-whisper, "Mommy wouldn't let me watch TV."

Eldon shook his head slowly. "Is that right, sweetie?" he said. "She won't let you watch TV? Well, just remember

137

that Mommy's doing this for your own good. Mommy wants you to have a chaste and untouched mind. You're uncontaminated! Don't you feel superior?" Alice wasn't quite sure what he was saying, but she was quite sure what he meant.

When we were ready to leave, and putting our coats on in the front hall, I gave Eldon Alice's test scores, which had come that day in the mail. He read them at once, and started to frown.

"Wait a minute," he said, as though I were trying to trick him, "What do these mean, Lydia? I can't tell what they mean. What's the bottom line here? How does she compare?"

"Her scores are average to slightly below average," I said, opening the front door.

"*Wait a minute, please*," said Eldon, anger in his voice. "Don't turn your back on me, Lydia. Don't walk out on this conversation. This is important. What do you mean, they're below average?"

I sighed. "I'm not walking out on this conversation. We have to leave now or we'll be late to the Laffertys'. I am assuming that you will be coming with me, and that we will continue the conversation on the way." I went out into the hall and pushed the button for the elevator. Eldon followed me, slamming the door shut behind him.

"I would like your attention for one minute on this matter," he said.

I turned to face him. "My attention is all yours," I said. The light was on, the elevator was coming.

"What do you mean, Alice's scores are below average?"

"They're not much below it," I said, "I called the school. Very slightly below average, two points, to be exact. And anyway that's only in the coordination part, manual dexterity and things like that. She's one point above average in one of the reasoning tests."

The elevator doors opened and I walked in. There were two other people in it, whom we didn't know. We all nodded at each other, polite but not friendly, and we rode down in silence: it was not the moment to discuss below-average test scores.

In the taxi Eldon started up again, his voice angry, as though the scores were my fault and I were a junior partner. "But *why* is she below average? Isn't there something we can do to improve her scores? Some program we can get her into?"

I looked straight ahead. "Not that I know of," I said. "She doesn't like doing the things that would help manual dexterity. She won't do the things that Sarah and I do— making collages, weaving, sewing, things like that. She gets impatient."

"Of course she gets impatient," Eldon said, "if she can't do it. Why wouldn't she get impatient? Can't you help her? Can't you do things with her that will improve her?"

I turned to Eldon. "Can't *you* do things with her that will improve her? Can't you do anything with Alice besides watch television with her?"

"That is completely unfair," said Eldon, furious. I said nothing, and sat back on the seat, looking straight ahead again.

"Why didn't you take her to the museum last weekend, for example?" I said.

"She didn't want to go. And, if you recall, I wanted everyone to come to the museum, not just Alice."

"Since Sarah was sick, and Flora was off, it made much more sense for you to take Alice alone. Instead of which you sat and watched television all afternoon, and Alice whined."

"That is *completely* unfair," he said again, but it wasn't, and I didn't answer him.

At the dinner party we kissed the Laffertys hello, and told them that we loved their new Irish walnut hall table. We gave our coats to the maid and ordered drinks and went into the long, rich-patterned living room where everyone was sitting, smiling and talking. Eldon and I split up and went to different groups, and didn't have to talk to each other or even look at each other again until dinner. Then we were seated catty-cornered across from each other, and during dessert we became part of the same conversation.

My dinner partner was Michael Darlington, a large, conservative blond man who loves gossip. He had told me with pleasurable surprise that the oil company responsible had discovered that the environment had not been damaged, as the environmentalists claimed, by an oil spill in Alaska, but had actually been improved. We marveled over this, and then moved on to the plight of the farmers who have to leave their inherited land and move to cities and become computer programmers.

I don't know why it is but farmers touch me. Just the thought of them, getting up early, early, in the dark, moving out through the quiet, cold air in their grimy jackets, turning on the lights in the barn, speaking to the waiting cows. Working slowly. It breaks my heart when I hear about them losing their land, it's as simple as that. Eldon thinks I'm a fool.

"But what do you think the government should do for the farmers?" Michael asked me, smiling around his dessert spoon as he slipped it into his mouth. I could see he thought I was a fool, too.

"Why shouldn't the government take some responsibility?" I said. "It was government farm programs that persuaded the farmers to borrow money and buy more land on credit, and buy expensive machinery and start using chemicals."

"And the farmers listened to the *government?*" Michael asked, his eyebrows raised in mock disbelief, his shoulders shaking with mirth. "They should have known better than *that!* My God! They deserve whatever they get!"

I had been keeping my voice down, trying to keep our conversation private, but Eldon must have been bored, or else he was waiting for a chance. He leaned over his dessert bowl toward me, and I knew I was in trouble.

"Why should the government subsidize the farmers?" asked Eldon loudly, his voice scornful. "There are lots of people out of work, Lydia. Why are the farmers so special?"

"Because farmers are different," I said. I tried to sound steady and balanced. "They represent something, they mean something. Farmers are a national resource," I said, pleased with the phrase. "And what they do is different from what other workers do."

"*How* is it different?" Eldon asked, insultingly.

"A farmer is making things grow, he's dealing with living things. He's dealing with life. He's creating it. It's important," I said.

"A factory owner is making his company grow. And he's dealing with living things—his workers."

"It's not the same," I persisted, but I was beginning to lose heart, not because I didn't believe what I was saying, but because Eldon was so angry. "A worker on an assembly line can learn his job in two weeks. It takes a lifetime to learn how to farm. And it's a commitment that this country needs. We need people who are dedicated to nourishing, and committed to their community. We need fewer people who are uncommitted, rootless, who don't care what they produce or where they live."

"Oh, my God. I wish Harvard Business School could hear this speech. Sweetheart, this is pure sentimentalism," said Eldon. Sweetheart is what he calls me when he hates me. And you would have thought, from his voice, that I had accused him of stealing. "Mom and apple pie. You want the government to set up programs to protect sentimentalism." There was such scorn in his voice.

I can argue with Eldon in private; if I get angry I will take him on dead center, but I can't do it when he attacks me in public. I shrivel inside, it makes me feel sickened, listening to Eldon talk as though he has nothing invested in this marriage, as though he takes pleasure in showing the world how pitiful I am, how worthless, and how intelligent and articulate he is. I lose heart, I can't argue back. I stop.

"You're talking nonsense," said Eldon. "You know nothing about economics, Lydia, nothing. Until you do, I suggest you stay out of conversations that concern them." He put down his glass with an air of great and elegant finality.

But for once I didn't stop. It seemed to me that something was wrong here. There seemed to be two levels we were talking on, two things we were dealing with, only one of which was acknowledged.

"Eldon," I said. "You are very quick to ridicule this point of view."

"Yes," said Eldon, and laughed. "Yes. I am. It's ridiculous."

"But you benefit from it," I said, "and so do you, Michael. Every man with a wife depends on her to take this point of view." They both looked at me, waiting. "If you came home, Eldon, and told me you'd lost your job, would you expect me to say, 'Well, dear, that's the capitalist system at work. You can't expect them to make exceptions for you. You must not be very good at your job, or else you haven't been working hard enough, and you should have been fired: that's how things work. You can't expect special treatment. Meanwhile,

I'm leaving you. I want a husband who's more successful. Economic Darwinism, you know—someone has to support me and my children'? Is that what you would expect me to say, Eldon?"

Michael had ignored me at first, eating his dessert discreetly and pretending not to hear us, because this had seemed to be a family squabble. Now he raised his head and looked at Eldon. He had a little grin on his face: he liked what he was hearing—it was so juicy—and he was changing sides. Eldon made a disgusted noise. He set his fork down and shook his head.

"Sweetheart, you're confused," he said. "These things have nothing to do with each other."

"They do," I said. Michael's grin had given me confidence. "At home, you expect me to be all warm and fuzzy. You expect me to be all *heart* in the private arena, where you benefit. You want me pure humanitarian, warm and sympathetic and loving to you. But the minute I bring those same responses, the ones you rely on, out into the public arena, you ridicule them. You ridicule them and you try to humiliate me for having them." My voice grew stronger. "You're standing on my shoulders, and pretending you're tall. And you're making fun of me for being short!"

Michael started to laugh, looking at Eldon, his shoulders shaking again.

"She's got you, Winthrop," he said, but Eldon just shook his head again and laughed loftily, as though what I had said was so idiotic as to be beyond discussion.

"You're in trouble, Winthrop." And, of course, being Michael, he couldn't resist going further, into private, gossipy, painfully intimate territory. He leaned forward toward Eldon and lowered his voice, delighted. "What's going to happen when you get home tonight? I wouldn't want to be in your shoes, I'm afraid," Michael said, shaking his head at Eldon, and still laughing.

Eldon now spoke to Michael, excluding me, laughing. "You may be right, Darlington." He sounded as though he were an adult discussing a child. "There'll be tears before bedtime, I'm afraid," he said, shaking his head, jocular.

I didn't go on. I was pleased with what I had said.

We kissed everyone good night, smiling and laughing, but once in the elevator we stopped speaking and our smiles died. At home we hung up our coats in the hall closet without touching each other. I went in to check on the girls, so Eldon didn't. In the bedroom we undressed without looking at each other. Once I brushed against Eldon as I was pulling my dress over my head and I apologized, as though the touch of my flesh would grieve him.

I was in bed before he was, propped on my elbow, reading. He climbed in next to me and turned off his light. He lay on his back and clasped his hands beneath his head, expansive with hatred.

"I suppose you think that was very clever of you," he said.

I didn't say anything. I did think it was clever, but I knew better than to admit it. I didn't want any more argument. I had said what I had to say. I wanted to read my book and then turn off the light and go to sleep. I didn't want anything to do with Eldon.

"Well?" he said.

I sighed. "You suppose I think *what* was very clever?"

"What you said at the Laffertys'."

I shook my head without answering.

"Lydia," he said, turning on his side toward me. I said

nothing, willing him not to touch me. "Answer me," he said. His voice was deadly.

"*What is it?*" I said, finally.

"How dare you say something like what you said?"

"How dare I?" I said, at once enraged. I was now so angry I turned over to face him. "What do you mean 'How dare I'? You do nothing but belittle me. Anything I say in public makes you smile. You get this little smile on your face, for 'the things that Lydia says.' You smile that way when you talk to Alice about me. 'Oh, did Mommy say that?' you say, as though 'Mommy' is another word for moron, and you and Alice know better. You treat me like a servant, like a whore," I said, and then my body betrayed me, and I could feel the tears starting, but I kept going. "Night after night after night you're away, traveling, or at business dinners. You're never around. You're not here. Then you come in late and want to screw. You treat me like your whore, as though the only thing that I do that can be of any use to you is fucking, and I hate it."

"Is that what you think?" Eldon cried, his voice raised. He was leaning over me as though he would kill me, his body a threat to mine. "Is that what you think?"

"*Yes, that's what I think,*" I said, hissing it into his face. I was beside myself now, with rage and with disappointment. I waited for him to hit me, and there was something in me that wanted him to hit me.

"How dare you talk to me like that," he said. He got up out of bed and went out of the room. I heard the water run in the bathroom. He came back and stood in the doorway in his boxer shorts, his hands on his hips.

"How dare you pretend that you're warm and sympathetic to me at home, as though your face lights up when

I come into our hall. How dare you say that in public, as though that's what you're really like. All you have for me is silence and anger," he said, his voice rising. "You give me nothing. *Nothing!* Do you think I *want* to travel all the time? Do you think I wanted a wife who treats me with scorn and sarcasm, who hardly looks up when I come home?"

Of course I was angry when he came home, how could I not be?

"Don't you think I would give anything to have you— have you—" but he couldn't finish that sentence. His voice chopped at the words, and then stopped, and I could hear something hard rise up in his chest.

This was a terrible moment. The fact that he couldn't go on was terrible. It broke me down, and my anger stopped. Something inside me broke down. I was frightened by the fact that he couldn't go on. I'd never known Eldon to stop in the middle of a sentence, for his body to betray him, and it was terrifying to see him break down in a way that I thought was female, was mine. But I was also frightened of what he would say if he did go on, it seemed as if I couldn't bear what would come next.

I'd never seen him desperate, and I could see now that he was. Seeing him trying to speak, trying to get the words out, hearing something rise up in his chest, cutting off his words, was a horror. It was as though he were having a heart attack. It *was* a kind of heart attack, and I had caused it. I could see then that I could destroy him. That I *was* destroying him, and that I had thought he was destroying me. And in the middle of this I thought of Alice: of how much I loved her. I thought of her being carried off by Flora, calling desperately to me.

And all these thoughts swirled inside my head, and

held me still, my heart pounding as though I myself were having a heart attack. I felt that same feeling of horror and peril and urgency. It held me motionless, half-turned toward Eldon, while he stood in the doorway, those terrible words still caught in his throat: what I had to do was to reach him before they came out. Neither of us could bear to hear them.

FRIENDSHIP IN A
FOREIGN COUNTRY

The house they have rented is on the grounds of a seven-teenth-century chateau in Provence. The long, graveled driveway is lined with dappled sycamore trees, casting a dry, rustling shade and letting through careless patterns of light. The chateau is made of golden stone, and stands squarely at the end of the drive: handsome, symmetrical, grand. The approach at first is formal, but at the last minute the drive swerves sharply to the right, skirting the chateau and ending in a quiet, shady courtyard behind it. Their own small house—*le Pigeonnier*, the dovecote—lies beyond this, through iron gates.

The two women would be alone together until the week-end, four days. They had arrived in the evening, and now they both sleep into the deep heat of the next morning. The sun beats on the thick walls of the house, coming through the cracks between the heavy wooden shutters, sliding in bright streaks across the walls, lying in fiery lines across the floor.

Sophie lies motionless in her bedroom, nothing on, spread-eagled across the square, white bed. When she opens her eyes, her mouth is thick with heat and sleep. Her room is large and shadowy, with windows, now shuttered, on three of its sides. A pair of French doors opens onto a tiny *balcon*, a place to survey the day. Sophie pulls on an old caftan and pads in to the bathroom; the terra-cotta floors are cool against her feet. Out of the small window she can see the peak of the dovecote, where the birds stalk about on the tiles, nodding and purring, brilliant white in the sun. Beyond them is the dry, green presence of the vast fig tree, and beyond that is the vibrating blue sky of Provence.

Still barefoot, Sophie goes into the shadowy hall. The other bedroom door—Louisa's—is still shut. Louisa's husband, Mack, is not joining them at the weekend, as is Sophie's husband, Peter. Louisa and Mack are getting a divorce. Louisa's new state seems to be reflected by her bedroom: it is much smaller than Sophie's, and it seems an admonition, a severe reminder of her new condition. The high, narrow window gives one point of view, the single bed has room for only one body, uncomforted. The admonition is not only social but economic: the closet is stingy, and the bureau has only two drawers.

Sophie knows very well how things are now for Louisa; she is barely scraping along. Her car insurance has expired, and she can't afford to fix the dishwasher. Another friend is paying for the dishwasher, and Sophie is thinking about making a general offer of assistance. When Sophie had first asked Louisa to share the house, Louisa had hesitated, and Sophie knew she was thinking about money. In the past, the two couples had rented houses together, always splitting the cost. But Sophie and Peter have made it clear that Louisa is invited as a guest. Sophie would like to make up, somehow, for Louisa's loss.

Sophie wishes that the inequity of things was not made

quite so tangible, so explicit, by the two bedrooms. The master bedroom boasts two closets, a big bureau. The bed is broad enough for war as well as love, and the room suggests procreation, expansion, the churning up of air and emotion.

Sophie goes quietly past Louisa's door and downstairs, past the dim, shuttered living room, and into the small white-tiled kitchen. She makes coffee, washes a furry peach, and goes outside under the grape arbor.

The sun is already fierce, but the vines make a bright patch of shade, a roof of vivid green. Sophie settles herself in one of the faded canvas chairs looking out over the terrace, past the dusty rosebushes. Beyond a stone wall are dry fields, and beyond those are the low sandy mountains that Van Gogh painted, thick with cypresses, hot and blue in the distance. Sophie looks out at them beneath the brim of her straw hat, her eyes half-closed against the glare, and wonders how the painter could have seen them so tumultuous, so wild. She wonders how he could have stayed awake long enough to paint them. She herself feels peaceful, dazed with sleep and heat, awash in the happiness of being there alone with her friend.

The two women have been friends for eight years, ever since they met in the Connecticut suburb where they both then lived, both married to Americans, both feeling foreign and awkward. Ever since, in fact, the morning when Louisa had called up Sophie and asked politely, "Could you tell me what a 'scrambles paddles' is? Or it may be a 'paddle scrambles.' We've been asked to one, but I don't know if it's a meal or a wife-swap."

Louisa—creamy, plumped-out, calm—is English. Sophie—thin, dark, uneasy—is half-French, half-American. There had been a third foreigner—another English girl,

Anne, though she was more Louisa's friend than Sophie's. Friendship in a foreign country is a different sort. You are tender, more generous, more forgiving. There is a secret alliance among you, and your only luxury is trust.

Sophie had been a solitary child—her parents had divorced early, and her mother had been a rambler. She did not make friends easily. She had been embraced by Louisa's warmth, entranced by her appreciation, her talent for celebration. She had fallen in love with Louisa. It seemed to Sophie that everything Louisa did was extraordinary. This was partly because of the way she looked: she was eccentrically beautiful, odd, amusing, with her long legs, her funny striped socks, her hats. But it was also her opinions, the books she read—everything about Louisa seemed original, to Sophie.

Sophie remembers her visits to Louisa's as charmed: the wide front door opens inward, and in the big hall Louisa stands, glowing. It is winter, and the house is warm, and smells of apple wood and pomander.

Louisa clasps her hands together. "Oh, good! How *are* you?" she asks, delighted, as though they have not spoken for months. She takes Sophie tightly by the shoulders and hugs her, pressing her smooth cheek against Sophie's, first one side, then the other.

"I'm so glad you're here, I haven't seen enough of you lately," she says. Linking her arm in Sophie's she leads her into the sitting room, where there is a fire, and a tea tray in front of it. When Sophie is settled on the rug, her teacup in her hands, Louisa leans toward her.

"Isn't that a new sweater? It suits you. You're very good at that. I never see you in something that doesn't reflect yourself."

"Thanks," Sophie says, "it's old, though."

"But very nice," says Louisa. "Now, tell. How was your trip to see your mother?"

This was, of course, the center of their friendship—the endless conversation about families, husbands, children, friends, clothes, books they were reading, how they felt. They told each other everything, and they agreed on everything: they found the same things shocking, the same things proper, the same things funny. It felt to Sophie that when she was with Louisa they were in a charmed and secret place, the two of them allied against the world.

When Louisa and Mack had moved, two years ago, to London, the conversations had continued, by echoing, expensive telephone calls, and through long, ruminative letters, but things are left out of letters and phone calls, and a great deal had happened that had not quite been explained, not entirely discussed. This visit was to knit them back into each other, to reestablish the connection, supplying the nuances, the things too intimate, too private, too difficult to write, or to trust to telephone cables.

Now Louisa appears in the doorway. She is, as always, impossibly white; she looks as though she had never seen the sun, as though her surroundings can have no effect on her. Her hair is thick and blond and very straight, chopped off flat at shoulder-level. Her narrow eyes are a brilliant blue, with long, pale, thick eyelashes. She is wearing a cotton *pareo*, tucked under her bare arms like a bath towel.

Sophie's heart lifts at the sight of her. "Good morning," she says, smiling at Louisa.

Louisa smiles back, beautifully, and gives a little wave, but does not speak. Sophie knows that Louisa doesn't like to talk in the mornings, not even the latest possible kind, like this. This is one of her eccentricities which Sophie cherishes.

Louisa sits down in her own canvas chair, her cup in her hand. When she has finished half of her coffee she is at last ready for speech, and she sighs blissfully. "Isn't this wonderful?" she says. "We have all week to talk."

"It is," agrees Sophie: she has felt starved for her friend.

"I can't tell you how I've missed you. I talk to you so often, whether or not you know it. We have long conversations in my head. But now you can actually say things on your own. What a treat!"

Sophie smiles, stretching her thin brown arms out in front of her. "Well," she says, "Here we are." They smile at each other, and Sophie begins. "Now, tell. What's it like being single again?" She feels sorry for Louisa, having to start all over, the indignities and misunderstandings.

Louisa puts her coffee cup on her lap, crosses her neat ankles, and considers. "It's very odd," she begins. "I suppose I do feel single, but not the way I did when I was a bachelor lady. I suppose you aren't really single if you have two children. You can't just chuck things and go off for the weekend with a devilish creature, and you can't take up with someone who doesn't like children. I feel very cautious, very measured—like an ocean liner—and I used to feel like a speedboat."

"And how do Jake and Lucy deal with it?"

"They take turns. If Jake is being horrible, then Lucy is charming, and vice versa. But usually Jake is desperately jealous, and Lucy acts like a little sister. She loves hearing stories about how the evening went. Once she came in to say good night when I was in the sitting room before going out. She came in in her nightie, all pink and damp and adorable, and shook hands with him first, and then came over to me. I could tell she was up to something, she was much too polite. She kissed me like an actress, on the cheek,

153

and gave this hideous photogenic smile, and said, 'Good night, Mummy.' I said good night, and then she leaned over and in the most tremendous stage whisper she asked, 'Mummy, is this the one with the bad breath?' "

"And was it?"

"Of course it was," says Louisa, sipping from her cup.

Sophie laughs. "You make it sound as though there are droves of them hanging around you, men I mean."

Louisa puts her head on one side. "Not exactly droves. But there are one or two more than I know what to do with."

"So there should be," says Sophie decidedly. She has been married for twelve years, and she wonders how it would be to have more men around than you knew what to do with. "I can't even imagine it." It makes her feel odd and uncomfortable.

"Well, you have to remember all your old tricks," says Louisa. "Like when you come back for a drink after dinner you sit in an armchair instead of on the sofa."

"Why?"

"Because they can't come and sit next to you in an armchair."

"Oh," says Sophie. "Mechanics."

"They're very useful," says Louisa matter-of-factly.

Listening to her, Sophie hears no regrets, no second thoughts, no self-pity. Louisa seems to move through her days without doubts: this is a marvel to Sophie, whose days are lit with anxiety. It is also a surprise, for she had thought Louisa would be riddled with guilt. And Sophie feels faintly backward, not having droves of men around her, and not even knowing something as basic as chair-choice. All this is confusing, because she had planned to comfort her friend.

"Well, I think it all sounds like heaven," Sophie says.

She wonders, surprised, if there is a tiny curl of envy in her voice. "I'd love to have an affair."

"Oh?" says Louisa. "Why do you want to have an affair?"

"Just for the thrill of it," says Sophie ingenuously.

Louisa waves her hand generously. "Well, then do. Have an affair. But *don't* get a divorce. Murder would be quicker and kinder."

"Is that how you feel? Like a murderess?"

"A bit."

This seems reassuring to Sophie—there is some cost involved, after all. They sit in silence.

"But you definitely can't go back to him, absolutely not?" pursues Sophie. She still hopes this will happen, and has never really understood why they split up.

Louisa shakes her head, closing her eyes. "I couldn't possibly. You have no idea."

"I know, you've told me," says Sophie carefully. "But you know, everyone is terrible to each other. Peter and I are beastly to each other, but it's not important. I mean, we know each other's beasts, and they're similar. There are things I couldn't forgive Peter for doing, or he me, but we have the same standards, so our beasts don't do those particular things."

"Well, that's it, then," says Louisa, "Our standards were different, Mack's and mine."

She has told Sophie the stories about herself and Mack. They shocked Sophie, not because of their content—everyone acts badly—but because of their implications: Sophie had thought that their marriage was perfect.

The first time Sophie and Peter had been invited to Louisa and Mack's, the four of them had moved into the sitting room after dinner. It was summer, and the long evening was still light in the meadow beyond the windows. As Louisa moved past Mack he had reached out and pulled her to him, and they had stood in silhouette against the soft, fading light. They were nearly the same height, and in silhouette they seemed part of each other. He had said something into her ear, and she had laughed. Witnessing it—the gesture, the whisper, the laugh—Sophie thought respectfully, *There. That's how it should be.*

When Louisa had told her that she and Mack were separating, it was that image—the two of them, joined—that had come to Sophie's mind. It seems mysterious to Sophie now, that this image should be false. She feels sympathetic, but baffled. And she also feels deceived, in a way.

"Well, you two seemed perfect together," she says now, flatly.

"Well, we weren't," says Louisa, just as flatly. "It was an act. We knew we looked perfect. It was part of what kept us together."

"But why did you never tell me things were so awful at the time?"

"I didn't dare," says Louisa. "It was all or nothing."

"Well, you fooled me. You seemed a lot more perfect than we did. I never even saw you have an argument. And God knows you've seen me and Peter have them often enough."

At the dinner table, in front of Mack and Louisa, she and Peter have, more times than she has liked, turned angry at each other. One shared ski weekend Sophie had energetically smashed several plates in the kitchen, as a prelude to her and Peter spending the night slamming doors on each other.

Louisa smiles at her and shakes her head. "Oh—fights. They don't matter. Just don't get divorced."

Sophie smiles back. "Oh, then I won't. But, tell about

you. Who's the main man now? What about this Michael Pollen?"

"A thing of the past, I'm afraid. He's too difficult for me."

"A change."

"It is. Mack's American difficult. He just wants everything his own way. Michael is English, very tortured and convoluted. It was too much for me."

"Well?"

Louisa settles down. "Well. The last time I saw him, we'd been planning a weekend, but it had been on-again, off-again. He kept changing his mind back and forth, very mysterious. He was full of apologies, very polite, but I had the feeling somehow that he liked changing back and forth. By Thursday we were on again, and we went out to dinner together. The children were already with Mack for the weekend, and I was supposed to be spending the night with Michael.

"We had a very nice dinner, very cozy, and we went back to his flat afterward. When we came in, he turned on the answering machine. At once a woman's voice came on, rather loud, and chummy. 'Hello darling, it's me,' she said. 'Listen, the weekend's on after all. I'm *frightfully* sorry about the muddle, but I couldn't help it, as you know. I'll meet you at the car on Friday at six.' Then there was a pause, and then she said, 'I don't know what woke you up in the middle of the night like that, but I hope it happens again,' and then there was another pause, and she hung up."

Sophie takes a deep breath. "God," she says. "What did Michael do?"

"He made a great show of banging the machine off, and shoving the table against the wall. But when he turned around, there was a tiny little smile at the corners of his

157

mouth. And when I saw that, I realized that he'd heard the message earlier. This was deliberate."

"A real sweetie," says Sophie. "So what did *you* do?" She is full of anticipation.

"First I thought, 'Right, I'm off.' "

"You just walked out without a word? Good for you."

"No. I thought I would, and then I thought, Why should I let him be in charge? That's what he wants me to do. I'll leave when I'm ready. So I took off my coat and started up the stairs. He just stood there, so, halfway up, I turned like Mae West and said, 'Coming up?' "

"You stayed?" Sophie asks. Now she is shocked again. "You spent the night with this bounder?"

Louisa nods with satisfaction. "I did. I spent the night with the bounder. I left the next morning and I never plan to see him again. But I wanted to leave on my terms."

"God!" says Sophie, but not in admiration. The story is a revelation to her, and it doesn't seem to be about the Louisa she knows. Part of what Sophie feels is admiration, for Louisa's refusal to be victimized. But part of her is repelled. This feeling is contrary to the way she feels about Louisa, and Sophie wonders if she is being unkind, judgmental.

Louisa does not reply. She tilts her head back with abandon and looks directly overhead, into the ragged-edged grape leaves and the hanging bunches of grapes.

"These will be ripe before we leave," she says, "and the figs are right on the verge. They're going to fall into our mouths when we stand under the tree. It's too good to be true, this place." She turns and looks directly into Sophie's eyes, inviting her to share in the delight. This is one of the things Sophie loves about her friend, but right then she finds it difficult to respond. She nods, without speaking.

In the late afternoon they take the little rented car into

St. Rémy. They park under one of the huge trees, and loaf along the sidewalks. The streets are narrow and shady, though the heat is fierce. Sophie and Louisa pause to look at glass canisters of lavender and thyme, at sweet-smelling soap and sachets. Louisa puts her nose all the way into the jar of lavender, closing her eyes and sniffing. "Heaven," she says peacefully.

Sophie is glad to have Louisa tuck an arm inside her elbow, pressing it against her side. Sophie is having a harder time than she had expected in bringing their friendship into sharp focus: it still seems blurry and undefined. She had assumed that they would fall at once into that deep twinhood they had shared in America, but they seem to be in some different place. She thought she had understood Louisa thoroughly, as well as you do understand people. She thought she knew how Louisa would behave, or feel. But now she was hearing things that seemed to alter, or even deny, her own knowledge of her friend. Certainly she had been wrong about the marriage, which had seemed so superior to her own. And she was beginning to feel that she hardly knew the woman who could turn on the stairs and ask, "Coming up?"

They push open the leather-padded door to the big church on the main square. Sophie likes churches, especially small-town ones. Inside, it is dusky and cool, with the lingering pungency of incense. They split up, wandering separately through the scented darkness. Alone in one of the dim chapels, staring up at an age-blackened painting, Sophie wonders what it is exactly that you can expect from friends. Surely the same standards as your own? And if someone doesn't share your standards, but loves you, what then? Are you allowed to judge a friend? How much, and how often?

Louisa, approaching, shakes her head firmly. "Dreadful,"

she whispers. "The most boring church I've ever seen." Sophie is again caught off guard: she would have said something nice about the peace here, the silence, the sweet-smelling dark.

"The real life is out here," says Louisa, pushing open the door and stepping back into the heat and sunlight.

They amble again along the sidewalk, stopping outside the Souleiado store, where they lean against the window and admire the stacks of rich-patterned cottons. The woman behind the counter, with her square face and shining short brown hair, reminds Sophie of Anne. "How is Anne? Have you heard from her?" she asks. Anne had moved into New York shortly after Louisa and Mack had left.

"No," says Louisa, "we've lost touch, actually."

"You have?" Sophie is again surprised.

It was Louisa who was Anne's friend, Sophie had known her only at second-hand. It had been Louisa who had told her how unhappy Anne was, and how, that last summer, Anne had waked up each morning already in tears, her pillow soaked before the day began. Sophie had assumed that Anne's misery was connected to her husband, Tug, who wasn't kind to her. Tug was dark-haired, sleek, and fancied himself irresistible to women. Sophie and Louisa called him Smug.

"Yes," says Louisa, "it's too bad." Sophie looks at her—there is something odd about her voice—but Louisa is wearing dark glasses, and looking straight ahead. It is difficult to read her expression.

"Well, I haven't seen much of her since they moved back to New York," Sophie says. "The last time I saw her was awful. We were at a charity dinner in town, and we were all sitting at the same table. Smug was drunk, and trying to look down poor Carolyn Howard's dress, who was sitting next to him. Anne was being very dignified and sitting up very straight, her head very high and regal. She was ignoring what Smug was doing, but she began to send him let's-go-home signals. He kept ignoring them, and finally she leaned across the table and said his name. He looked up at her and said loudly—and contemptuously—'Look, if you want to go home, why don't you just get up and go the fuck home? I'm staying. I happen to be having a good time.' And he turned back to Carolyn's cleavage. Anne stood up instantly, as though she hadn't heard him. Her face never changed, she looked very dignified, and she left. Mack went and got her a cab. And Smug kept after poor Carolyn."

"How awful," says Louisa.

"It was awful," says Sophie, "only something even worse happened next, so poor Anne was sort of hidden by another layer of awfulness."

"Which was?"

"I told you that Tim Perkins got married again? To some poor young woman? Well, he was there, with his new wife. He was drunk, and after dinner he went up to Dick Connelly and said, 'Dick, I want you to meet Linda. She has the best tits in New York City. Linda, show him your tits.' And his wife had the good sense to pick up an empty wine bottle and hit him over the head with it."

"No!" says Louisa, "That *can't* be true!"

"It does sound implausible," agrees Sophie, and they both begin to laugh. This reassures Sophie: they do, after all, find the same things terrible, the same things funny.

Farther along the street they pause at the window of a small dress shop. A neat black silk dress, quite chic, is on display.

"Let's go look," says Louisa. Inside, they move along the racks idly, holding things up, considering. The prices are surprisingly high. The woman shopkeeper watches them.

She is trim and dark-skinned, a Provençal with a lined, energetic face and tired bronze hair. Sophie finds something to try on, and steps behind the curtain strung across the back of the shop.

It is the black dress in the window, short and tight. Sophie comes out to use the big mirror. She stands in front of it and piles her dark hair on top of her head, which gives her sharp face an aristocratic lift. She eyes herself coolly, her bright dark eyes, her brown shoulders and long legs. She twirls, consideringly. She likes herself in the dress. It is astonishingly expensive. The shopkeeper nods at her, affable, encouraging.

"Very nice," she tells Sophie.

"You think?" Sophie asks, still looking at the mirror.

"Oh, yes," says the woman, "very chic." She folds her arms tightly across her chest and nods again.

Sophie cocks her head, considering. She is really only wasting time, but the fact that the dress is so expensive piques her interest. It is, in fact, much more than she likes to spend on clothes. Anyway, she thinks, it would be tactless to buy it in front of Louisa, who couldn't afford it herself.

Louisa appears behind her: she is in the same dress, and has found a broad-brimmed black hat. She poses for them, her hands on her hips, her head thrown back. She cocks an ankle, smiling, showing off, teasing.

"Oh-la-la," says the shop woman, coming to life. "Voila!" She claps her hands together.

Sophie makes room for her friend, in fact she steps aside, relinquishing the mirror altogether. Louisa sweeps in front of her and takes another pose, one hand at the brim of the hat. She is laughing at herself; at the same time, she looks wonderful, and knows it. Sophie sees at once that this is how the dress should look: filled out, fulfilled. Against Louisa's moony, pale skin the silk is voluptuous, with mystery in its blackness. Louisa's milky shoulders are irresistible. Behind them, Sophie catches a glimpse of herself, her small, brown, heart-shaped face, her pointed chin and ragged hair, loose and stringy from being piled up. She looks like an orphan. Louisa smiles engagingly at herself in the mirror, the deep brim of the hat shadowing her face. She catches Sophie's eye and smiles. Sophie has a base thought: *she can't afford it.* She takes some ignoble pleasure at this. She is quite sure, now, that it is envy coloring her thoughts.

"It looks wonderful on you," Sophie says bravely. "I'm not sure it's quite right for me." She hopes for contradiction.

Louisa turns and inspects her carefully, putting her head on one side and frowning. "No," she says kindly, judiciously, "I think you're right. It's not your style." She turns back to her own image and shrugs her shoulders charmingly. "But I'm afraid I have to have it for myself."

Sophie is dumbstruck. "Really? You saw the price?" The car insurance, she thinks, the furnace? The price of the dress is nearly half the house rent.

Louisa smiles. "You know me! Hopeless about money. Don't have it, must spend it. Hopeless, but there you are." She shakes her head and shrugs her shoulders again. The shop woman begins fussing, smoothing the folds over Louisa's shape, loving the dress on Louisa. She looks up.

"The price, Madame?" she says, "I could give you some reduction on the price, if you would like."

"Oh, could you? That would be so kind," Louisa beams at her. She speaks very good French, for an Englishwoman. Her accent is charming, and the cadences are right. The shop woman has fallen in love with her, and she clucks, nodding.

"Oh, yes," she says, and hesitates. "Madame," she asks, "are you—well known?"

"I don't think so," Louisa says, laughing. "How do you mean?"

"You are not a movie star, someone famous?"

Louisa shakes her head, radiant. "Not yet," she says.

"You have something," says the shop woman, smiling at her, "a certain air."

Invisible, Sophie goes back behind the curtain to take off the dress. Alone beneath the shimmering black folds she wishes suddenly that Peter were coming before Friday.

Back in the street Louisa begins to hum, her step jaunty and ebullient. She takes Sophie's arm again, but now it seems awkward, and, anyway, Sophie thinks, it is too hot. She holds her arm aloof from her body.

They pause before a real estate window to look at the photographs: regional farmhouses, either grand, with cypresses and swimming pools, or more modest, with only a grape arbor over the doorway as an amenity.

"No," Louisa says finally, with great certainty. "They're all either too tarted up or too austere. The French aren't good at cozy. Except for you," she adds, hugging Sophie's arm. Sophie smiles but says nothing. She is in distress.

"Let's stop in at a cafe," Louisa says. "I need a drink to get my nerve up." She steers them along the main circular street, lined with sycamore trees and cafes.

Sophie is feeling peculiar. She is feeling something very close to rage. She is afraid that she is resentful and envious of her best friend. She doesn't want to feel this way at all, but she does.

They sit down at a sidewalk cafe, and Sophie looks at the people at the next table. She does this to keep from thinking about Louisa, this person who, it seems, is someone she hardly knows at all. Next to them is a family: a black-haired, hatchet-faced man, Italian-looking, and his short-haired, fair-skinned wife, English-looking. Their two restless daughters, in long ruffled skirts, kick their legs under the table. All of them look grumpy: clearly this is not how they envisioned their holiday. None of them speaks. The parents watch the steady stream of small cars in the street, the girls stare sullenly straight ahead, kicking resentfully.

It is five o'clock; Louisa orders a Campari soda. Sophie stirs her *citron pressé*, and watches the sugar cloud up in a slow swirl. "Why do you need to get your nerve up?" she asks. She does not want to look at her friend.

Louisa shakes her head. She gets out her cigarettes: the polished ebony case, the silver art deco lighter. This is one of the things Sophie has always admired about Louisa—the things she uses every day are old, treasured, beautiful. Now, the lighter and case seem pretentious, and the habit vile. Louisa flicks the lighter against her cigarette and draws a long breath through the tobacco. It is an elegant gesture, and Sophie is reminded, against her will, of what it had been like to smoke—the pleasure of it, the voluptuous, irresponsible pleasure. But she is suddenly furious at Louisa for smoking.

"You must stop," she says coldly.

Louisa nods agreeably. "I must." There is a pause.

"Well?" Sophie says finally. She is feeling more and more distant from Louisa. They live, after all, on opposite sides of the Atlantic Ocean. There are, between them, thousands of miles of cold, shifting tides.

"It's something you don't want to hear," says Louisa, diffidently. She is not smiling. Sophie wants to shrug her shoulders, turn away. She almost says, "Then don't say it." She imagines herself explaining to someone, offhand, "Oh, we just lost touch."

At the next table the two little girls begin kicking at each other under the table, their ruffled skirts swinging with their efforts, their eyes still fixed in front of them.

"Well?" Sophie makes herself say again.

"I've often wondered if you knew. I thought you did," Louisa says, speaking slowly. "I always wanted to tell you, but it didn't seem to be something I could say over the telephone, or in a letter."

Sophie waits.

"All right, then," Louisa says, but instead of going on she takes a sip of her Campari soda. Sophie is surprised: whatever it is, it is difficult for Louisa.

"Tug Simmonds," Louisa says finally, looking first down at her glass, then bravely up at Sophie.

Sophie stares at her, blank. Anne Simmonds's dreadful husband? "Tug Simmonds?" she repeats, stupidly. Louisa nods, and from her expression—embarrassed and pleading—Sophie suddenly realizes what Louisa is announcing.

"You and Smug?" she asks, horrified.

"I don't, actually, call him that," says Louisa gently.

"Louisa," says Sophie. She can think of nothing else to say. She sees Smug's confident smile, his bold, possessive stare. She thinks of fragile Anne, waking up in tears. She seizes on a straw.

"But they moved to New York," she protests, as though this would make Louisa take back what she said.

Louisa nods. "That's when it started."

Sophie definitely does not want to hear how it started, the first looks, the first touch, the rapturous yielding. She feels like throwing up.

"Does Anne know?" she asks.

Louisa nods again. "I'm afraid so," she says. "It was awful. Talk about a murderess."

Sophie looks at her, then away. At the next table, the littler girl aims a tremendous kick at her sister's thigh. Her sister twists agilely away. The littler girl misses, and the momentum carries her off her seat, and she slides under the table and onto the floor. Her mother turns at once and speaks sharply; the father glares. Sophie listens, automatically, to hear what language the family speaks, to find out who they are, but in fact she feels sickened, and does not want to know, right then, about other people's lives. She stirs her *citron presse* some more. She does not want to look at Louisa.

"Does Mack know?" she asks, wanting to remind Louisa of things: trust, promises, responsibilities, commitments. Sophie's heart goes out to Mack.

Louisa nods meekly. "It's all over now," she offers, and Sophie, looking at her for the first time, sees now that it was Smug, not Louisa, who had ended it. She sees that Louisa hopes she will sympathize with her, but Sophie finds it difficult.

"What was it between you?" Sophie asks finally. Perhaps she had missed something about Tug Simmonds. Perhaps he was, really, terribly kind, brilliant, and shy.

"It was mostly physical, I'm afraid," says Louisa apologetically. She has stopped being charming, and has become subdued. Her head is down over her drink: she is waiting for her friend's judgment. In her voice there is pain and humility. Louisa is waiting for her friend to forgive her; Sophie feels unequal to the task.

She stares into her drink, rucking up the sugar, putting things off. At the next table, the mother and the father speak angrily to the younger girl, and the older girl, who has been trading vicious kicks with her sister, suddenly defends her. Talking back defiantly, she first takes her sister by the hand, then puts her arm around the younger girl's shoulders. The child leans against her sister's chest, watching the angry grown-ups, safe.

Now Sophie remembers the morning after the fight on the ski weekend. She and Louisa had gone off to buy groceries in Louisa's little Volkswagen through the glittering landscape. Sophie, humiliated by her own behavior, had finally brought it up. She apologized for the broken plates, the slamming doors, the fury, all the broken shards of civilization she had been responsible for. Louisa had been cheerful and reassuring. "You mustn't worry about it once it's *over*," she kept saying, shaking her head, smiling. "Don't go on thinking about it."

But Sophie could not help but think about it. She felt she had done some terrible, irretrievable damage, losing control, screaming. She felt disgraced, that what she had done could never be forgiven.

"I thought," she said finally and painfully, "that when we came downstairs this morning that we'd just find a note from you and Mack, and that would be the last we'd see of you." She stared miserably ahead at the snowy road.

Louisa's response had been instantaneous. She had braked the car so quickly that it skidded, and they slid gracefully, giddily, on and on along the dazzling white surface, safe between the high banks of snow on either side. Louisa had paid no attention to the car or the road. She was looking at Sophie, and her hand was locked around Sophie's wrist.

"Never," she said gently, and it was the surest sound Sophie had ever heard.

So Sophie, stirring her *citron pressé* under the great sycamore tree, waits. It is up to her, she can see that. Louisa has given her the compliment of her trust—she need not have told her at all. And Sophie reminds herself that everyone is beastly now and then—passion makes sure of that. There are things we do even against our wills—falling in love, feeling envy. There are things that have no place in friendship, and judging is one of them.

So Sophie waits, stirring her drink slowly, until she can find the tone she wants for her voice. When she has found it, she will look up again at Louisa, who is her friend.

GRADUATION

❧

I drove up on Friday to Jeffrey's graduation. I went alone: Alex, Jeffrey's stepfather, was away on business and couldn't come till Saturday. St. George's is in Rhode Island, just past Newport. It's a four-hour trip from Manhattan, but I didn't mind the drive. The afternoon I left, I stood in the garage on Eighty-third Street, waiting for the attendant to bring my car. I started breathing deeply, big, long breaths, and I closed my eyes, as though I were standing in a windy meadow and not on the oil-stained concrete floor of the garage. I couldn't help it: I couldn't wait to start. I couldn't wait to be in the car, I couldn't wait to begin the racing surge along the smooth highways, every second drawing me closer to Jeffrey. If you have only one child, that child is at the heart of your life.

I reached St. George's around six. The school is on a wide hillside overlooking the ocean, and everything glitters with the light off the water, and the air is fresh with salt. The school buildings are red-brick Georgian with white trim, set with big old sugar maples. It was a clear day, early summer, with no wind. By the time I got there, shadows were stretching across the sloping lawns, turning the landscape majestic. Driving up the long driveway, I felt peaceful to be at this place, so calm and handsome.

I found Jeff in his room. It smelled rank, as always—a rich mixture of healthy young men, dirty socks, and industrial cleanser. And everything they owned—clothes, shoes, athletic equipment, electronic parts—was all in a great swirl, across the floor, on the beds and desks, in and out of the closets, like debris after a flood. It looked wonderful. My own room I want immaculate, each chair set in its own footprints on the carpet, but I love Jeff's room like this. It makes me laugh, all that energy.

Jeffrey was sitting on the bottom bunk bed, fiddling with his Walkman. He is tall now, and lanky, and his joints make odd angles. His limbs seemed to fill up the whole rectangle of the bed. He looked up and smiled when I came in. Each time I see him it is a tiny shock: he has come to look more and more like his father. In between, I forget this, but when I see him next it hits me again. Jeffrey has Bill's wide square face, short straight nose, his odd low eyebrows and muddy blond hair. In fact he looks exactly like his father when I first met him in college. It is a face that I once loved, and one which now makes my heart shrink.

I leaned over and put my arms around those smooth, strong young shoulders, closed my eyes, and willed the face to change into my son's again.

"Hi, Mom," he said.

I sat down next to him on the bed. "Well, I'm glad to see everyone's all packed," I said cheerfully, looking at the voluptuous heaps littering the room.

Jeffrey grunted, he had gone back to the Walkman. His roommate, Owen Schaefer, appeared. Owen is impossibly tall and thin, with no-color short hair that stands straight up from his forehead. He has been Jeff's best friend since freshman year, and I am a great fan of his.

"Hi, Mrs. Winslow."

"Hi, sweetie, how are you? Come over here and let me give you a kiss." Owen permitted this. "Are your parents coming up, I hope?"

"No, Mom, they're busy. They can't make graduation, they have a party this weekend," said Jeff, not looking up from the Walkman. I rolled my eyes and shook my head at Owen.

"Thank you, Jeff," I said, and Owen laughed. "What's the matter with the Walkman?" I asked Jeff. "The batteries?"

"No," said Jeffrey, his voice making it clear that the problem was too complicated for a maternal sensibility.

"He probably needs a new one," offered Owen solemnly.

"Right," said Jeff, pleased.

"Thank you, Owen," I said, and we all three laughed.

Jeffrey may be at the heart of my life, but I am not at the heart of his. I was, of course, when he was little. At first, you are your child's whole, whole world, and though you love him, though he is at the center of it, he is not your whole, whole world. For years the child is like a beloved anchor, dragging on you, slowing you down. He pleads with you constantly: to play with him, read to him, help him out. You do it, of course: you are all he has, and you love him. But infinitesimally and inexorably, things shift. When he is fifteen, you realize suddenly that the burden, the debt, has slid heavily and forever onto the other side, like the ball of mercury in a thermostat. Now you have become the supplicant: for the rest of your life you will be asking him to spend time with you, and feeling grateful when he does.

Jeff is eighteen, and my affection makes him uneasy. I don't care: I love him and he has to put up with it. When we first heard that he had gotten into St. George's, I said, "That's wonderful, sweetie! And I'll get a little apartment in Newport! I love Newport."

Jeffrey shook his head. "Very funny, Mom," he said. I could see him wondering if I was going to be one of those mothers who turn up too often, wearing the wrong clothes and saying mortifying things about rock music to his friends. I haven't done that. But this is how I feel: his presence in my life is huge, crucial, heartrending, in a way that mine will never again be in his.

Now Jeffrey keeps me at a distance, but he's supposed to: he's an adolescent boy. It means he's establishing himself as a separate person, not that he hates me for divorcing his father and marrying Alex Winslow.

I'm waiting for things to get better, and they're not so bad right now. There are times, like then, sitting next to Jeffrey on his unmade bed, in the wonderful chaos of his room, and being conscious of his smooth skin, the tender young bristles on his upper lip, the easy, supple strength of his limbs, breathing in the fresh, strange smell of him, and laughing with him and his roommate, when I feel so grateful I want to close my eyes. I wanted more children, but I am so glad at least that I have this one, so thankful to have been able to start a life like this: a miracle.

Jeff and I went out to an early dinner. I took him back to my hotel, in case he wanted to talk or watch TV or something after dinner. The hotel was one of the old Newport mansions, and the rooms were handsome, oversize, and gloomy. We were alone in the dining room, and we took a table next to the ocean wall. We sat on either side of a cold, black window. We could feel the draft coming from it, and beyond it we could hear the invisible sea on the rocks. I looked around—at the long, ponderous curtains, the dim reaches of the ceiling, the solemn classical archways dividing the vast room.

"Can you imagine living here?" I said. "It's not what I'd call cozy. I hope they didn't have to have breakfast here every morning."

I was trying to stir Jeff up, but he just looked around and smiled. He didn't say anything. He drank some of his water.

"When you get back, we'll find a camp outfitter and take a day to get all your things for Alaska," I said. He is going kayaking this summer in Prince William Sound.

"Okay," said Jeff.

"Your trip will be so great," I said. "I want you to know that we never did things like that when I was your age. You went to Camp Wikkee-o-kee, in Maine, every summer until you were seventeen. After that you still went every summer, only then you were a counselor. No one ever asked us if we wanted to go kayaking in Alaska or trekking in Nepal or helicopter skiing in Cortina. In fact, *still* no one asks me," I finished up. I was sure Jeff would challenge me on this, as my childhood was not deprived, but he didn't. He laughed, but didn't answer. He was pretty quiet: I knew what was on his mind.

"Well, Alex is flying in early tomorrow. And your father and Susan, they're coming up tomorrow morning too?" I asked carefully. He never mentions his father to me, not ever.

"Yup," Jeff said.

"And you're having dinner with them tomorrow night," I said.

"Yup," said Jeff. This made him visibly uneasy, so I didn't ask where they were going.

"And then Alex and I will take you out to lunch on Sunday."

Jeff was eating carefully, watching his plate. His foot jiggled steadily under the table, a tiny, febrile throb. How could he not be uneasy? The next day we would all be there together, Bill and Susan, his new wife, and Alex and me and Jeffrey, which has never happened before. I was dreading it myself.

Bill and I have been divorced for four years, and he is still full of rage. He hasn't spoken to me in two and a half years; all communication is through lawyers, accountants, or his secretary. His secretary includes brief notes about plans when she forwards my school mail (there is some continuing mixup, and periodically the school sends my mail to Bill's office).

Last spring vacation Bill took Jeff skiing in Austria. By the terms of our agreement we are supposed to share Jeff's holidays. Bill was going to take him for the first week, and Alex and I would take him to Nassau with us for the second. The day Jeff left for Austria, after we had said good-bye, he stopped in the doorway of our apartment and turned. He was wearing his big red parka. His bag and boots were already on the elevator, and the car was waiting downstairs to take him to the airport. He put on one of his mittens, and jabbed at the door frame with his blunt mittened hand as he talked. He looked at the mitten instead of me.

"Mom," he said.

"What is it?" I asked. "Do you need money?" He seemed so troubled.

"No," he said, not looking up. "I'm not coming to Nassau."

"What do you mean?" I asked.

"Dad said he'd only take me skiing if I'd come for the whole vacation, both weeks. And he said I had to be the one to tell you. He said he wouldn't. He got really mad." Jeff spoke without raising his eyes to me, banging away at the door frame with his mitten. For a second I just stood there—I couldn't believe what I was hearing.

"But why didn't you tell me?" I asked. "Why did you wait until now to tell me?" My voice was angry.

Jeff's mitten stabbed at the brass door socket. "I don't know," he said resentfully.

But I went on. "What do you mean, you don't know? You knew I'd find out, Jeffrey, why didn't you tell me?" Unexpectedly, I began to cry, which I think I have never done in front of Jeff. I swept the tears off my cheeks with the backs of my hands.

"I didn't *want* to tell you!" Jeff said finally, looking up at me. He saw my face, and his own face crumpled. "Because I knew this would happen when I did," he said, and then, horribly, his voice broke, and darling Jeff, my large, sweet-smelling, kind Jeffrey, began to cry, too.

The car was waiting downstairs to take him to the airport. There was nothing for me to do but let him go. I put my arms around him and told him that it was all right. I told him to have a great time skiing, and that I loved him. What else could I do? Bill is good at getting what he wants. I knew how he had acted to Jeff: threatening and jeering, alternately. He's a bully, it's one reason I left him.

When they came back from skiing, of course I tried to reach Bill, but he would never take my calls. Finally my lawyer wrote a letter of complaint, but Bill never responded. My lawyer reminded me that the law is expensive and cumbersome to set in motion, and he asked me what, in the end, it was that I wanted to achieve? What I want to achieve is never to have Jeff put in that position again, and so now I let Bill do mostly what he wants. I suppose I hope that being placating will finally earn me absolution. In any case it will protect Jeff.

Bill's secretary sent the graduation information to me with a note saying that Bill wanted to have dinner with Jeff on the Saturday night after graduation. I suppose that night is the climax of the weekend, but I didn't argue. Anything is better than putting Jeff in the middle.

When Jeff and I left the hotel dining room he said he didn't feel like coming upstairs. He said he had to pack, which was visibly true, so I drove him back to school. When I stopped the car outside his dorm he didn't move or look at me. I knew what he was thinking, and I wished I could make things easier for him.

"Don't worry," I said, "it won't be so bad."

I hugged him. When he was small, things seemed so easy: I could make things whole and right, simply through the fact of my presence, my body. Things are different now, I am forty-two, and can no longer count on my body to do the things it used to.

Over his shoulder I could see the lights of the dorm, brilliant in the dark landscape. There was all that life in there, music thudding and doors slamming: that was where Jeff's world was now, not in my arms. He was too polite to pull away, but I could feel him aching to, to disconnect from me, so I pulled away first.

"Good night, sweetie," I said, "I'll see you tomorrow."

He opened the car door. "Good night, Mom," he said, "thanks for dinner." I nodded, and as he shut the door I waved to him as I started the car, and I drove off at once, so it wouldn't look as though I were yearning, wistful, abandoned.

When I got back to the hotel Alex called, from wherever he was.

"How's Jeff?" he asked. They are great friends, thank goodness.

"He's worried about tomorrow. Surprise."

"How about you?"

"I'm all right," I said. "Hurry up and get here."

"Don't worry," he said.

I read for a while and went to sleep. I felt fine that night. It was the next morning when I began to worry.

I woke up alone in that big bed, and anxiety closed down over me like a poisonous fog. I ordered breakfast, and got up and dressed, but it got worse. I stood in front of the mirror and my heart sank: how could I have bought this suit? Jeff would be embarrassed; Bill and Susan would laugh. It looked awful, but there was nothing else to wear. I turned from the mirror and went to stand in front of the window.

Why wasn't Alex here by now? Wasn't he late? Was he all right? I wondered if something had happened to him. No one would know where to find me, if it had. I wouldn't know until I got back home on Sunday. These things were skittering about on the top of my consciousness: I was trying to avoid the big things.

I was afraid that Bill would do something terrible, something public and humiliating, something that would discredit me as a mother. I couldn't think what it was he might do, but it was in my mind, like the nightmare when you have no clothes on in public: shame and degradation. I was worried that Jeff would be caught in the middle again, that he would be trapped, bullied, blackmailed into taking his father's side against me. I was afraid that his own graduation, instead of being a day full of pride and exultation for him, would be one of anguish and misery.

And then there was another thing, unconnected to what Bill did to Jeff or to me: why was it that Susan had had a baby, easily, at once, getting pregnant after one month of marriage, at the age of forty-one? I had tried to have more children, first with Bill, after Jeff was born, for the next eight years of our marriage. Then I had tried with Alex, for the four years of ours. I tried everything, everything. I started with pills and injections and unnatural couplings, and worked my way up to anesthesia, operations, terrible glittering steel and glass, bloody changes to the center of me. I let them do things that hurt, that went too deep. I didn't mind anything, though, I was greedy for it all. Each time I rode along on a high, blissful wave of conviction, until I was told once again that I had failed, my body had betrayed me again.

In the mirror I could see that my neck was thin, my skin was becoming parched. I was forty-two, and on the wane. The flow in me was subsiding. I would never have another baby. This whole part of me, this delicious current, this heavenly voluptuous flow of passion, this blissful, legitimate, uncomplicated tide of love would have only one object, ever. I would never have a whole enchanted circle of faces that were mine, that looked for me, that gave themselves up to me entirely, that needed my face for the completion of their world. I would never hold a baby on one hip, another small body leaning easily against my legs, a third rocking unsteadily toward me. It was what I had wanted; it wouldn't happen. That part of my life was gone, was over.

I try not to think about this—it does no good—but there are times when it hits me and the air seems to turn dark around me, as though I am in mourning. Then panic rises up in me: I am afraid that I will give way, that I will let this dark wave break over me.

I sat down now on the bed and folded my arms against my chest. "No," I said out loud, firmly. I held my arms tightly, pressing in hard. "No."

There was a discreet knock on the door: "Room service."

It was Alex. He stepped inside and gave me a big, slow, enveloping hug. All of him wrapped around me and squeezed. It felt wonderful. Alex kissed me and then stepped away.

"Don't you look terrific," he said.

"Really?" I asked, starting to laugh. One of the wonderful things about Alex, besides, of course, his generosity of spirit, is his sideways approach. He knew perfectly well that it wasn't the way I looked that was on my mind.

"Yes," he said, studying me carefully and nodding. "Susan will turn green when she sees you."

The graduation was in the gymnasium, and Bill and Susan sat on the other side of the room. Alex and I sat with Owen's parents, Jim and Libba Schaefer. The four of us clapped dutifully, and laughed at the jokes, and kicked each other when the hated French teacher was introduced. I yawned suddenly and horribly during the visiting dignitary's speech, and Libba poked me, and we both turned weepy when our sons stepped forward for their diplomas.

After the class marched out again we all began to follow them outside. Everyone was milling around on the lawn, and we inched our way through the crowd trying to find Jeff, and watching for Bill and Susan out of the corners of our eyes.

"There he is," I said to Alex, and we ploughed toward him. He was talking to the parents of a friend. His face was

cautious, his hands busy rolling and unrolling his diploma.
He seemed so nervous, I felt sorry for him. I threw my arms
around him and kissed him.

"Congratulations, sweetie," I said. Alex hugged him, too,
and Jeff's smile broke through. I introduced myself to the
other parents, and we stood talking for a few minutes. I stood
on tiptoe the whole time, trying not to let my heels sink into
the soft lawn. My peripheral vision was in high gear. Bill
and Susan were behind me, to my left, talking to someone
I didn't know. They were edging their way toward us, and
I could feel the back of my neck turn prickly. I wanted to
be calm, I wanted to overwhelm them with poise, with ami-
ability. But as I could feel them coming nearer I could feel
my body beginning to subvert me. My pulse had speeded
up, and I was having trouble breathing. Nothing seemed to
work normally, and my face was turning stiff, I wouldn't be
able to smile. Even moving my mouth to talk felt peculiar.
I could feel them coming nearer.

I turned to Jeff and said, "We've told the Schaefers we'd
all eat lunch together, I hope that's all right with you?"

"Uh," said Jeff, nervously.

"With your father and Susan, of course. I'm going to go
find the Schaefers and get a table. You collect your father
and come find us."

"Okay," said Jeff, without a flicker, and just as Bill and
Susan arrived I fled. I nodded at Susan, but just barely, it
might have been part of my turning away from Jeff. We
made our way back to Jim and Libba. My ankles were shaking, from standing on tiptoe I thought, but my hand, holding
the program, was shaking, too. My heart was pounding, and
my whole peculiar body, without my permission, was in a
state of wild alarm, as though I had had a near miss with an
axe murderer.

But, miraculously, it turned out all right. At lunch we all sat at a round table. Jeff was between me and Bill. Alex sat next to me and Susan next to Bill. Jim Schaefer sat dutifully next to Susan and Libba next to Alex. Between the Schaefers was Owen. I subdued my nervous system. It was very civilized, and I was very proud of everyone. The two sides never had to speak to each other, and Bill and I let Jeff turn back and forth from one to the other in spurts. We were all animated—manic, really—and I could see Susan being charming, irresistible to Jim Schaefer. Alex is always charming, and he made Libba giggle. In an odd way, it wasn't too bad. It was excruciating, but it wasn't too bad: there we all were, sitting together, and nothing terrible had happened. Bill had done nothing after all. I thought, if this is the worst, it isn't so bad.

That night Alex took me to the most expensive restaurant in Newport, where we had too much to eat and too much to drink, and a lovely time. In the morning we made love, and so we were late to the chapel service, and had to stand in the doorway.

The chapel is small, graceful, and Gothic, and it was packed. I never even saw Bill and Susan. Jeff was next to Owen in the choir stalls. I thought how simple young faces are. The boys looked so clean, so handsome and tidy; they had somehow managed to spring, immaculate, from that chaos they lived in, as they had emerged from the long, rumpled, complicated, chaotic process of childhood. Here they were at last, beautiful, loved, capable, ready to live their lives. It was a miracle.

Standing there, listening to the lovely, high, soaring voices asking "And did those feet, in ancient times," I felt exhilarated. It was partly relief: it was such a vast blessing to feel that it was over. Nothing had happened, we had all been polite, and maybe things would go on getting better. Maybe at last I had been forgiven. It was so lovely there, all of it, the rows of smooth, young faces in the choir, the high ceiling soaring over our heads, the pure white plaster walls, the hymns: it seemed enchanted. I thought, this is our reward, this is all we hope for, starting these children off, and it's more than enough.

Afterward Jeff hurried past us in a group of boys, his head down. He didn't see us, I guess, so I reached out to grab him.

"Wait a minute, Mister," I said. "Not so fast. Good morning," I leaned forward for a kiss but he ducked. It was too public for him, so I patted him on the shoulder instead.

"Oh, hi," he said, nervous. "Listen, I have to go. These are Owen's pants. He needs to have them back, they're leaving right away."

I looked down: Jeff's white pants were rolled up over his ankles. "Oh," I said. "Why do you have Owen's pants, or is that a silly question?"

Jeff sighed elaborately. "Mine got red paint on them, remember? Now I've got to go. I'm keeping the Schaefers waiting."

I pushed him easily away. "Go," I said. "We'll come find you in your room."

We made our way there slowly, stopping to talk to people we had come to know in four years of Parents' Weekends. It was a triumphal procession. There were the favorite teachers, whose faces lit up when they saw us, who loved Jeff themselves, who honored our love of Jeff. There were the other parents, whose children had shared this school with Jeff, these four awkward, long years. We were happy to see one another, like survivors after a war. It was over, we had all succeeded. We all felt congratulatory, proud of one another and of ourselves.

Near the dormitory I saw Libba. I waved to her and called, "We're keeping the pants. They're much nicer than Jeff's."

She laughed, and as we came up she put her hand on my wrist. "Listen, I never saw where you were sitting last night," she said, "but I wanted to tell you how fabulous Jeff's speech was."

I stared at her. "Last night?" I said.

"At the dinner," said Libba.

"At the dinner," I repeated. "What dinner?" My heart started up again, pounding away like a fool. I didn't know what she was going to say, but I knew I didn't want to hear it. I didn't want this to go any further.

"What do you mean 'what dinner'? Here at the school, dummy," said Libba, "The senior class dinner. Jeff's speech was *wonderful*. Had you heard it before? Of course you must have. You must be so *proud* of him."

I stared at her, and I couldn't do it. I couldn't cover for myself, I couldn't think of any way to fill that terrible black space she was creating. I couldn't think of a sentence that would show that things were all right, that I had known this, that her words weren't scraping at the core of my heart. I couldn't do it. I just stood there and stared at her, and finally she realized what had happened.

"Oh, no," she said, and put her hand on my shoulder. It was too much, and I pulled back.

"Listen, we've got to arrange with Jeff about the car," I said loudly, "we'll see you later." I pushed ahead again, as though everything in the world depended on my getting through this crowd. Alex was next to me. I didn't know whether he had heard or not, but I couldn't tell him. It seemed as though they were words I could never say out loud, sounds that would kill my heart if I ever heard them again.

When we reached the dormitory we started down the hall, but there was a group milling around Jeff's room. As we got closer we could see what it was: Susan was standing in the doorway, right in the middle of it, so no one could pass by her. In her arms was a baby, Bill's second son. Susan held him with one arm; she had him propped easily on her hip, and her other hand was outstretched. She was smiling at Jeff's friends and introducing herself. "Hello, I'm Mrs. Carpenter," she was saying—my old name. As I came up she was shaking someone's hand and smiling.

"Good morning, Owen. Congratulations! Now, there's someone I want you to meet. You haven't met Graham, Jeff's little brother. Say hello, Graham," she said comically.

She turned to the baby, and jiggled him up and down, easily, as though she were used to having a baby on her hip. Then she picked up his small pink hand and made it look as though the baby were waving, saying hello to Owen Schaefer, my friend Owen, who stood there smiling back, who had shaken Susan's hand; Owen, who had betrayed me.

GETTING ON

&

Priscilla's husband began bleeding very late on New Year's Eve.

This was not the result of wild partying: they had been in bed by ten. Mary McDougal had served them an elegant meal: smoked trout, roast veal, lemon soufflé, and two very nice wines. Edward had toasted Priscilla, lifting his glass and inclining his head courteously. "Priscilla, dear," he said. "Edward," Priscilla said, lifting hers, and they drank together.

"Well, what shall we do with this one?" Priscilla asked, leaning back as though she could see the year standing before her like an old cabinet, each drawer full of possibilities. She was seventy-three years old.

"I plan to do a lot of errands. Catch up on sleep. Find God. Things like that."

"I have *lots* of plans," Priscilla said grandly. "I want to put in white iris, all along those granite rocks. I have a vision of a great drift of white against that dour gray stone. And I think this is the year for the rose garden. I want it along the bottom lawn, against the fence. I plan to become known as the first great blind landscape architect." Priscilla had, in spite of three operations, lost almost all of her sight two years earlier. She now wore thick glasses, which made her eyes look bleary and enormous beneath her short, tufty white hair.

"Purr," Edward said, "why don't we just have roses sent out by limousine from New York every day all year? It would be much cheaper."

"Edward—"

"A rose garden would cost the earth," Edward said. "It really would. You'd have to bring in nearly two tons of topsoil, and gravel and things. I looked into it once. And here's Mary with the champagne, which I'd much rather have than topsoil and gravel."

Every year Edward asked Mary McDougal to sit down and have dessert and champagne with them. She had been with them in the house in Connecticut for sixteen years. He always drank a toast to her.

"To Mary," Edward said, raising his glass. He was small-boned and frail, and dry as a cricket. "We could not do without you." He was a kind man, gentle, but not sentimental.

Mary McDougal, neat, sandy-haired, and Scottish, dipped her head.

"We *adore* you," Priscilla announced. She took a long drink of champagne and raised her glass again dramatically. "Having you here makes it *pure* heaven. Being without you is impossible to imagine—pure hell, I'm sure." Priscilla had been outspoken since she had learned, early, to talk.

"To both of you," Mary said, raising her glass and nodding, with a small frown to show her seriousness. They were all three rather formal people.

"What I love about you, Mary, is the way you *learn*

things," Priscilla said. She looked at Edward. "Take Mary's birds. She knows a hundred times more birds than I've ever thought of. And she's only been at it about a minute."

"Eight years," Mary said.

Priscilla waved her hand. "I've been at it for thirty," she said, "or meant to. The way I go after things like that is to put the book under my pillow and sleep on it, hoping that something will seep through during the night. Mary really learns all the different calls, and the colors of the mates, and every little thing. It's *quite* extraordinary. I'm still stuck on crows and robins."

Edward smiled. He would not be drawn into his wife's hyperbole. He was a dry counterpoint. "Quite extraordinary," he said.

"Do you know we had two downy woodpeckers at the feeder this morning?" Mary said, uncomfortable at the praise.

"They're cold," Edward said. "We should be putting suet out for them."

"I have been," Mary said. "It was four below zero this morning."

"Dear God," Priscilla said, "why didn't anybody tell me?" She was six feet tall, and had been lean and rangy until her forties, when she was attacked so violently by arthritis that she considered suicide. Instead, cortisone had been discovered, and Priscilla had chosen relief over vanity. Her body was now bloated and blurred by the disease and the drugs, and she shuffled about the house with a walking stick. She went outside rarely during the winter.

"It's bitter," Edward said, looking at his wife. Edward's skin was a very pale tan, and his eyes were a dark, bright brown. He spoke flatly, without inflection, and he seemed to be in possession of some quiet secret that other people did not have. Calm and complete, he watched other people steadily as they spoke.

It was just before ten when the three of them went off to bed—Mary McDougal to her room off the kitchen, Edward and Priscilla to the other end of the house. Edward went alone up to the big square bedroom he and Priscilla had shared for thirty years. Priscilla now slept in the guest room off the library, which had become her room when she could no longer manage the stairs. Neither slept immediately. Edward was rereading *War and Peace*, and he looked forward to this thin strip of distant turbulence and remote passion before he slept. Priscilla watched the news on a television set perched right next to her bed. She could see very little of it, but she knew each of the voices, and she could see gestures and make out some of the closeups. It comforted her to find this familiar group available to her night after night. She turned off the television after the news and slept, her thickened body a large mass beneath the peach-colored covers.

In the middle of the night, Mary McDougal knocked gently on her door. Priscilla was a light sleeper and awoke immediately. It's come, she thought calmly, though she did not know what she meant by that.

"What is it, Mary?" she asked, sitting up.

"It's Mr. Green," Mary said. "He's bleeding. From the nose. I've tried ice, but it won't stop."

"Have you called the doctor?" Priscilla asked. She struggled to disentangle her feet from the bedclothes.

"They're sending an ambulance," Mary said.

"Would you hand me my wrapper?" Priscilla had gotten free, and swung her heavy feet onto the rug.

"Are you going up to him, then?" Mary said, her accent strong.

"Of course I'm going up to him. Would you hand me my cane, please?"

When she reached the bottom of the big front stairs, Priscilla called up, "Whoo-oo! Edward! I'm coming up!" She put her foot onto the bottom step, gave her cane to Mary, and took hold of the banister.

By the time she had reached the landing the ambulance had arrived. Four men in pale-blue shirts and dark-blue pants carried a long stretcher up the stairs, angling around the corner. "Excuse me," one of the men said as they stepped smoothly past her. Priscilla wavered and turned toward Mary.

"It's the men with the stretcher," Mary said loudly. "Let me help you down. We'll wait in the hall."

The two women made the trip down carefully, step by step. By the time they reached the hall, the men in blue had caught up with them. They carried the stretcher as though it weighed no more than before, as though it were worth no more than before. They started to go by the two women, but Priscilla, leaning forward onto her cane, stopped them.

"Just one moment," she said loudly, as though she had caught them stealing something from her house. The men stopped; Priscilla shuffled to the stretcher. "Edward?" she asked, as if hoping that he were still upstairs, unconnected with these strange, crisp men.

"I'm here, Priscilla," Edward said, and he reached out a hand and touched her forearm in the woolly robe. The rest of him lay passive: he had given other people responsibility for his movement.

"*There* you are," said Priscilla, as though she were reassuring him of that. She could not make out her husband's face; the stark white of the sheets seemed uninterrupted. She patted his hand. "Don't worry," she said, her voice strong.

"Don't *you* worry," Edward said. His wife peered toward his voice, trying to discover his face. It was muffled with wads of Kleenex. Edward had taken a whole boxful and pressed it to his nose; he had not wanted Priscilla to see the blood.

"We've got to get back to the vehicle," said one of the men in blue.

"Yes, all right," Priscilla said. She wished she could see Edward's face; she wished she could stoop easily and kiss him before the men carried him out the door. She patted his hand and stood back, releasing him. The men walked on with the stretcher, making no noise at all on the thick, dark rugs that stretched the length of the hall.

"I'll get you some warm milk, shall I?" Mary said loudly, speaking to cover the sound of the front door closing behind the men.

Priscilla heard the worry in Mary's voice, but liked to prove people wrong about herself. "No, thank you, dear," she said briskly. "I'll just take a pill and go right off to sleep."

The doctor had said only that things were under control, and that he would talk to her in the morning. Priscilla took her pill and lay in bed in the dark, waiting for the pill to work. She had timed it: it took forty minutes to seep into her bloodstream, to quiet her thoughts. She hoped Edward had been warm enough in the ambulance—how cold had Mary said it was? But of course the ambulance would be heated.

She rolled heavily over to look at the time. She used a kitchen clock, with enormous numerals that glowed with an unholy green light. Even so, she had to turn on the lamp and reach for her glasses. Only fifteen minutes had passed. Priscilla had never thought Edward would leave first; the doctors had always been called for *her*. She had assumed he would go on looking after her: foolish, she thought now. He was six years older than she was, and there they were, three old people in a big house in the country. It could not go on forever. At least Mary would not leave her. When Mary had first come to them, she was in her early forties, and Priscilla worried that she might marry and leave them. Mary had been pert and unpredictable then, and never said where she went when she spent the night out. But that had passed. She was quieter now; the three of them would be childless forever. Priscilla had warned Edward in the very beginning that she could not have children. A clumsy doctor in Paris had settled that for her in 1932. Edward had said it didn't matter; what he wanted was her. He had never mentioned it again. She thought of her husband's kind silence. She wished she could have stooped and kissed him good-bye; she wished she could have ridden in the ambulance with him, holding him steady against the curves.

Priscilla shifted her feet under the sheets, wondering if she should take off some covers, or put some on. For a moment she could not remember what season it was, whether she should feel hot or cold. But it was cold, she remembered, with exasperation at her muddleheadedness. Edward had said it was bitter; she had worried about his being cold in the ambulance. She still could not really connect Edward with the ambulance—it was so unlike any way she had ever known him. But she had heard the door close behind him, she had felt the cold air come in around her. Surrounded by smooth flower-printed sheets and soft blankets, she tried to imagine the night just outside the walls of her bedroom, the still cold eating into the bones of the landscape.

*   *   *

In the morning, Priscilla asked Mary to put a call through to the hospital even before she brought in the breakfast tray. The doctor was precise, but he did not give Priscilla what she wanted to hear. Closing her eyes while she spoke to him, she wanted a particular tone in his voice, a note that would answer the question she was not ready to ask. But the doctor's voice was low and full of moderation. Edward was in intensive care; they were doing everything they could.

"Is he still bleeding?" Priscilla asked.

"Yes," the doctor said, "but very little."

"Why did he start?"

The doctor cleared his throat. "It's hard to say exactly," he said. His voice had shifted to a higher level, as though he were talking about something he took no responsibility for, something that sailed free through the air. "With someone that age often things just give out. Some of the veins in his nose simply gave out."

"But why doesn't it stop?"

"Your husband is taking medication for his heart that has an anti-clotting agent in it."

Priscilla thought about this. "So he's a hemophiliac."

"Practically speaking, the conditions are similar."

"Why can't you stop the heart medicine, for God's sake?"

The doctor sounded nettled. "We have, of course, considered that, Mrs. Green. We don't want to do anything drastic."

"What *have* you done?"

"We've cauterized the vessels and closed them. Another has opened, very slightly. We're going to give him a massive transfusion. He's lost quite a lot of blood."

"A transfusion, good," Priscilla said. She waited, but the doctor had nothing more to say.

A Glimpse of Scarlet

Priscilla had her breakfast on a tray in the dining room instead of in bed. She felt she must make a show of strength, that she must carry all this off.

It was still very cold, Mary told her. The trees were glittering with ice. Priscilla had to ask Mary to draw one of the curtains against the glare that fell across the table. She had tea, then toast, and part of a sweet green melon. She wondered what Edward had had for breakfast. Surely he was conscious? She could not bear to think of him with tubes entering his body.

She liked the idea of his having a transfusion. She imagined a huge vessel of blood blooming by his side, the steady scarlet stream flowing into his pale arm, enriching his frail body, urging him on. She had had a transfusion once herself, after the operation in Paris. It had been amazingly casual. On one side of a curtain lay a dock-worker, or a grocer, with black hair and a huge burly chest and a thick reek of garlic. She lay on a pallet on the other side of the curtain, and his blood flowed silently into her. She had felt wonderful afterward, rich and strong.

Priscilla drank her second cup of tea very slowly, sip by sip, as though the process itself were very important. She felt as though she were walking on ice of exquisite fragility, and that every step must be superhumanly smooth—a gliding gesture, without shock or impact. She did not want to turn her head suddenly, she did not want a thought to enter her mind unannounced.

It was particularly good tea. She preferred black Lapsang souchong to the stronger Earl Grey that Edward had liked. *Likes*, she corrected herself, frightened by the past tense. The trouble with Lapsang souchong was that it should be drunk clear and dark, the taste untroubled by milk and sugar, but Priscilla liked milk and sugar in her tea. It was a problem.

This morning she was having Earl Grey, with a little milk and a lot of sugar. She could tell from the feel that it was in one of the Herend cups, with butterflies on the sides and beetles in the bottoms of the saucers. She liked the butterflies, but had never been fond of the beetles. When Mary came in to clear away, Priscilla said, "We must send over a basket to the hospital. Some Earl Grey tea, some marmalade. What else? Should we send over whole meals, do you think?"

She tried to talk to the doctor again, but he was making his rounds. She left her name, and shuffled into the library to watch the news. The television was hidden by a pair of cupboard doors in the paneling; she sat in a leather arm-chair in front of it. Priscilla watched the news, then the soaps. She knew Mary was watching the soaps in the kitchen. At lunch they would compare notes. The people in the soaps were invariably badly behaved. "Wasn't it awful how he took up with his wife's sister?" Mary would ask indignantly.

Priscilla did not like the way the day was proceeding. Ordinarily, she could feel Edward's day traveling along next to hers. He might spend the morning reading, or writing letters, or out in the car doing errands, but she could feel the pace of it; she knew she would meet him for lunch, and for dinner. Now she felt him hidden and distant, his day unknown. This was the other part of his being in the hospital. The first part, grief and fear, she thought she could deal with, but this absence was more difficult, as it did not lessen. There was something at the back of her mind, but she did not seek it out.

On the third day, she had Mary drive her over to see him. She was wheeled through the long, quiet corridors, as though she herself were a patient, but this did not bother her. She wanted to get to him quickly, faster than she could walk. All her life she had wanted to get on with things.

Once in the room, Mary had to point Edward out to Priscilla, there were so many unknown shapes and outlines before her. When finally she could see Edward, she knew she had lost him. He had been taken over, closed off to her. There were vessels hanging over him, with pale fluids that dripped into the secret places inside Edward, not the direct red flow she had imagined but a slow, relentless drip. Sheets were spread over him, and his face—although she could not be sure—seemed smaller, the dry, parchment skin useless for expression or protection. Only the eyes were the same: dark, bright, watchful.

But Priscilla was herself. She had been preparing for this. She was a richly embroidered charmer—intricate, lush, inexhaustible. "Darling!" she cried, as though they were lovers meeting in front of the cameras. "You look very uncomfortable," she went on, turning her head, tilting it, to focus. "What can we do to make you feel better? And what would you like us to bring you?" The room was already bright with flowers. "I've brought your little radio, so you can have some good music, and some marmalade, and some Earl Grey, and a little pillow that smells good, and your silk pajamas . . ." Priscilla carried on as if she were in a salon. She did not know how else to behave. Edward smiled at her, and sometimes spoke. When Mary wheeled Priscilla out again into the hall, Priscilla felt as though she weighed three hundred pounds. She did not speak to Mary until late that night, when she asked if Mary would call the nurses' station to tell Edward good night from her. Then Priscilla took her pill and went to bed. The weight had not left her; she could barely move. It was an immense relief to settle down on the mattress and lie still.

*　　*　　*

Edward was Priscilla's second husband. She had loved Dennis, her first, with a headlong desperation that had not calmed in the fifty years she had known him. She had put him out of her life entirely, but when she thought of him it was with the fierce, remembered appetite of an addict. Dennis had stiff reddish-brown hair—they wore it short in those days—and wild blue eyes, and had been as trustworthy as a kite. He had made ardent love to Priscilla in Paris, while still married to his second wife. Once divorced, he had married Priscilla, and they moved back to New York. She had come home one afternoon to find him taking a steamy bath with one of her friends. She had never felt so outraged—that was really the word for it. All her love, all her high, keen passion, all that profound tenderness she felt for him, and the best he could do in response was to soap Julie Langdon's back up into a creamy lather.

Dennis had been even more ardent in winning her the second time than he had been the first, but she knew him now. During his siege, Priscilla met a friend in the middle of Park Avenue one day, and, balancing between streams of traffic, asked her friend what she was doing.

"Going to Reno to get a divorce," the friend said.

"I'm coming with you," Priscilla said, and that was that.

Edward had not swept her off her feet. He had waited for her. At parties he watched her, and he would smile, but he would not come over to speak. The first time he took her to dinner he picked up her hand and said, "These paws are enormous. Why do you have such large hands?"

"I'm six feet tall, that's why," Priscilla answered. She had been charmed: other men told her how lovely she was. Why was Edward so sure of himself? It was only from his close, silent scrutiny that she knew how he felt.

Priscilla was living then in a little apartment on East End Avenue, with windows on the river, and good rugs, and her beautiful Queen Anne highboy. Edward had sent her, carefully wrapped, a pair of shiny black galoshes with red buckles. They were huge; they must have been for a fireman, she thought. She filled them with freesias and lilies and put one on either side of the highboy. Edward smiled when he saw them, and nodded, but neither of them mentioned the boots.

It beguiled Priscilla that Edward would not be mad for her. She could not make him do what she wanted. Once, depressed and surly, she had hung up on him when he called. He had not called back. After a week she called him, anxious.

"Edward? It's Priscilla."

"I know that."

"Well, aren't you sorry?" she asked.

"For what?"

"For not calling?" Priscilla's heart pounded. What if she were going too far?

"Haven't I called?" asked Edward.

"Not enough," said Priscilla, and it was an apology. It was the end of her struggling; she liked knowing she had met her match, and she felt that Edward was kind and solid. Edward was for keeps, not for other ladies. He had been the center of her life for thirty-five years, and took all his baths alone.

When she lost most of her eyesight and stopped talking or moving, sitting like a fallen tree in the library all day, Edward had bullied her back to life. "Oh, there you are," he would say. "Still sulking. Good, good. Gets the blood going. Well, let me know if you ever want to say anything."

In the beginning, she had barely heard him. She could

not spare any extra attention, with the world turned into this shifting screen of smoky images, watery colors, and unpredictable shapes; she could not remember why people had conversations at all, or what there might be to discuss. Then she began to hear him, and she got cross and answered back. "I am not sulking, Edward, for God's sake. I'd like a little peace and quiet once in a while."

"Yes, I see that. I'm very impressed. Well, anytime you'd like a little conversation, do let me know."

She was sleeping downstairs by then, and that night he took her in his arms when they said good night to each other, holding her for a minute and breathing into her ear. She had been beautiful as a young woman; she knew why Edward had been drawn to her, but what could he now feel for the thickened, gimpy, bleary-eyed creature she had become?

Lying in bed, Priscilla realized that Edward would not come back to this house. However long it took, she could see that he had begun something which would end with his death, and that she was no longer connected with his life or even with this process of dying. She was now alone for good, in the big house with Mary. Edward would not emerge from the lemon-colored bedroom upstairs, he would not argue with her anymore about politics. Her life would be discussing the soaps with Mary, and listening to Great Books on her tape machine. Most of her friends had died, and her two brothers lived in California and Florida.

Priscilla rolled over in the dark, waiting for the pill to work. She would not think about that. Thirty years ago, she and Edward had bought twenty acres in this town and built a house. They had used it on weekends until Edward retired, and then they moved to the country altogether. The house was on a plateau. The land in front sloped gently down from the terrace, through marshes and meadows toward the road, which was hidden. In back, there were broad fields, and then the land began to rise to a wooded ridge, with glacial outcroppings of gray rock. Priscilla and Edward had planted very carefully. They had begun with a line of trees along the edge of the woods—redbuds and dogwoods and witch hazel—so that the first hint of spring was the mist of color at the end of the field, a fine haze that made Priscilla's heart lift when she saw it. She imagined the rest of the woods behind it, the oaks and ash trees building up slowly into a green breaker that would flood over the ridge and down across the meadows. The fields were full of jonquils and narcissus in the spring, and she had planted wild flowers in them for midsummer and fall: Indian paintbrush and Queen Anne's lace, chicory and sweet everlasting. Priscilla went over all of this in her mind.

Below the terrace was the lower lawn, and it was here that Priscilla wanted the rose garden. She began to plan it. She would have one long bed, the length of the lawn, with a wooden fence behind it for the climbers. She began to list the roses: Queen Elizabeth and Charlotte Armstrong, Albertine and Souvenir du Docteur Jamain. She had always wondered who Docteur Jamain was; she imagined a dark-eyed lover whose roses flourished on the strength of his passion. Along the fence she would plant New Dawn, Étoile de Hollande, Ophelia. She loved the names, and the flimsy softness of the petals. She wanted big bowls of roses, big floating pools of scent throughout the house. In the darkened room, she raised her hand above her head and opened the fingers, closed them. It was a small movement, and one that caused her no pain. She could do it easily.